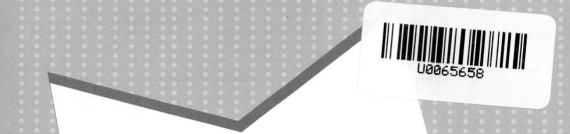

公 職 精 選

to win a prize

3 7 回 歷 屆
必 考 試 題

The essential 3000
words in public service
exam

字彙題 01

1. Mary loves weekends. Saturdays and Sundays are her_____ days of the week.
   (A) cold (B) favorite (C) difficult (D) possible

2. Grandpa discovered his surprise birthday cake_____ in the oven.
   (A) putting (B) eating (C) hiking (D) baking

3. Mountain climbing can be_____ because accidents do happen.
   (A) boring (B) effective (C) expensive (D) dangerous

4. I looked everywhere for my car key, and I finally_____ it in the bathroom.
   (A) avoided (B) ignored (C) found (D) arrested

5. Christmas is coming. Who wants to go with me to the_____ to buy the presents?
   (A) department store (B) movie theater (C) elevator (D) school

6. The President is going to_____ his new plan in the press conference.
   (A) inform (B) open (C) unveil (D) rebut

7. Please check out the_____ of our last meeting for the decisions made by our committee members.
   (A) minutes (B) miniatures (C) ministries (D) minuets

8. Rescue teams_____ the fire scene for signs of victims.
   (A) scored (B) scoured (C) scowled (D) scraped

9. Measures need to be taken to_____ the effect of inflation on the global market.
   (A) obscure (B) diverge (C) mitigate (D) multiply

解答 01

1. 瑪莉喜愛週末，週六及週日是她一週中最喜歡的日子。
   (A) 冷漠的 (B) 最喜愛的 (C) 困難的 (D) 可能的　　　　**B**

2. 祖父發現他的驚喜生日蛋糕正在爐子上烤。
   (A) 放置 (B) 吃 (C) 健行 (D) 烘烤　　　　**D**

   金榜解析 discover可接現在分詞片語做為被動語意的受詞補語。

3. 登山可能是危險的，因為意外確實會發生。
   (A) 令人厭煩的 (B) 有效的 (C) 昂貴的 (D) 危險的　　　　**D**

   金榜解析 do於肯定直述句中表示加強語氣。

4. 我到處找我的汽車鑰匙，最後終於在浴室找到它。
   (A) 避免 (B) 忽視 (C) 發現 (D) 逮捕　　　　**C**

   金榜解析 everywhere 到處
   = here and there

5. 聖誕節要到了，誰要和我去百貨公司買禮物？
   (A) 百貨公司 (B) 電影院 (C) 電梯 (D) 學校　　　　**A**

   金榜解析 coming 快到了
   = around the corner

6. 總裁即將在記者會中把他的新計畫公諸於世。
   (A) 通知 (B) 打開 (C) 揭示 (D) 駁回　　　　**C**

7. 請看一下會議記錄中，我們在上次委員會所做的決議。
   (A) 會議記錄 (B) 縮圖 (C) 部長 (D) 小步舞曲　　　　**A**

   金榜解析 make a decision 決定
   =decide

8. 搜救隊搜遍火災現場為了找尋罹難者的蹤跡。
   (A) 得分 (B) 搜尋 (C) 怒視 (D) 擦傷　　　　**B**

9. 我們需要採取措施來緩和通貨膨脹對全球市場的影響。
   (A) 隱藏 (B) 分歧 (C) 緩和 (D) 增加　　　　**C**

   金榜解析 take a measure 採取措施
   have an effect on 對…產生影響

10. When you are reading a novel for pleasure, you don't need to
_____ a dictionary for every new word you meet. You can
always guess its meaning from the context of the sentences.
(A) analyze (B) examine (C) investigate (D) consult

11. As former colonial powers, many European nations have plenty of
experience pacifying communities in conflict without immedia-
tely_____ to violence.
(A) catering (B) diminishing (C) resorting (D) acquiescing

12. When justice_____, it means that good overcomes evil and that
light conquers darkness.
(A) descends (B) prevails (C) perishes (D) declines

13. I have to study for my math exam. I don't want any _____.
Please do not talk to me or play loud music.
(A) negotiations (B) restrictions (C) observations
(D) disturbance

14. At busy intersections, _____ should cross the street via
underground passages.
(A) refugees (B) leaflets (C) pedestrians (D) pedestals

15. Mr. Stevenson always _____a sense of genuine interest in his
students. No wonder his students like him so much.
(A) condemns (B) condenses (C) converts (D) conveys

16. My father and his partners' cooperation is based upon their
_____ respect and understanding.
(A) drastic (B) hostile (C) mutual (D) pleasant

10. 把閱讀小說當作消遣時，你不需要逐字查閱新字，可以藉由句子上下文來猜測其意。

(A) 分析 (B) 檢驗 (C) 調查 (D) 查閱 　　**D**

金榜解析 **consult a dictionary for new words** 在字典查閱新字
=look up new words in the dictionary

11. 許多歐洲國家以往有豐富的殖民經驗，善於避免以訴諸武力的方式，調節團體之間的衝突。

(A) 迎合 (B) 減少 (C) 訴諸 (D) 默認 　　**C**

金榜解析 **plenty of** 許多＋複數可數名詞或不可數名詞
resort to violence 訴諸暴力

12. 當正義抬頭時，表示正派戰勝邪惡，光明征服黑暗。

(A) 傳下 (B) 占優勢 (C) 滅亡 (D) 下降 　　**B**

13. 我必須用功準備我的數學考試，不要打擾我，也請不要和我談話或大聲彈奏音樂。

(A) 協商 (B) 束縛 (C) 觀察 (D) 打擾 　　**D**

金榜解析 **play music** 彈奏音樂

14. 在交通繁忙的十字路口，行人應該經由地下道穿越馬路。

(A) 難民 (B) 傳單 (C) 行人 (D) 底座 　　**C**

15. 史蒂文生老師總是對他的學生表達出真誠的關注，難怪學生如此喜歡他。

(A) 判罪 (B) 濃縮 (C) 轉變 (D) 傳遞 　　**D**

16. 我父親和他父母的合作乃基於他們對彼此的尊重與了解。

(A) 激烈的 (B) 敵對的 (C) 互相的 (D) 愉快的 　　**C**

金榜解析 **based on** 根據
= according to

17. The economy is in bad shape, one reason for which is the rising _____ rate.
    (A) recreation (B) production (C) unemployment
    (D) enhancement

18. She looked immensely _____ when she learned that her son had survived the crash.
    (A) relieved (B) dedicated (C) upset (D) indignant

19. Please do not _____. The waste bin is just around the corner.
    (A) litter (B) query (C) smoke (D) talk

20. After she had the cosmetic surgery, the doctor reminded her to avoid any _____ to the sun.
    (A) devotion (B) exposure (C) reaction (D) sensation

考前衝刺★★★★★

1. The _____ of calcium may cause osteoporosis, and the patients may get bone fractures easily.
    (A) frequency (B) proficiency (C) deficiency (D) adequacy

2. The _____ of this button is to make sure we can stop the machine if things go wrong.
    (A) function (B) intention (C) collection (D) decision

3. Steve was _____ with joy when he found he had won the first prize in the lottery.
    (A) established (B) overwhelmed (C) equipped (D) suspended

答案

17. 經濟狀況不佳，其中一個原因是持續上升的失業率。

    (A) 娛樂 (B) 生產 (C) 失業 (D) 增強 　　　　　　C

18. 她得知自己的兒子已從車禍中活下來，似乎卸下了心中的一
    塊大石頭。

    (A) 安心 (B) 奉獻 (C) 不安 (D) 憤怒 　　　　　　A

19. 請勿亂丟垃圾，垃圾桶就在角落那裡。

    (A) 亂丟 (B) 詢問 (C) 抽菸 (D) 談話 　　　　　　A

20. 整形手術後，醫生提醒她要避免任何的曝曬。

    (A) 獻身 (B) 曝露 (C) 反應 (D) 知覺 　　　　　　B

考前衝刺★★★★★

答案

1. 缺乏鈣可能導致骨質疏鬆症，患者也可能容易骨折。

   (A) 頻率 (B) 精通 (C) 缺乏 (D) 適當 　　　　　　C

   金榜解析 calcium 鈣
   osteoporosis 骨質疏鬆
   fracture 折斷

2. 這個按鈕的功能是要確保萬一有差錯時，我們能夠停止機器運作。

   (A) 功能 (B) 意圖 (C) 收集 (D) 決定 　　　　　　A

   金榜解析 make sure (that) ＋子句 確保

3. 史提夫發現他贏得頭彩時欣喜若狂。

   (A) 設立 (B) 壓倒 (C) 設置 (D) 懸掛 　　　　　　B

公職精選歷屆
必考字彙題

4. The city now looks very artistic and refreshing because it is
   _____ with many colorful and well-crafted sculptures.
   (A) affected (B) decorated (C) excluded (D) generated

5. A laptop, an MP3 player, and a cell phone are often considered as
   _____ equipment for the generation raised in the age of
   technology.
   (A) extinct (B) expressive (C) elastic (D) essential

6. In this age of globalization, when people have more chances to
   travel, it is a great _____ to speak more than one language.
   (A) penalty (B) heritage (C) prejudice (D) advantage

7. Joe is really _____ about the party tonight. He's making lots of
   preparations to make sure everyone can have a good time.
   (A) envious (B) enthusiastic (C) concise (D) curious

8. This child has been _____ by his parents for a long time because
   they have been too busy working.
   (A) neglected (B) developed (C) grasped (D) connected

9. Keep in mind that smoking is strictly _____ when you are
   handling explosive materials.
   (A) eliminated (B) extracted (C) terminated (D) prohibited

10. Research shows that only some animals are able to _____ in the
    wild after being released from the zoo.
    (A) decrease (B) express (C) prevent (D) survive

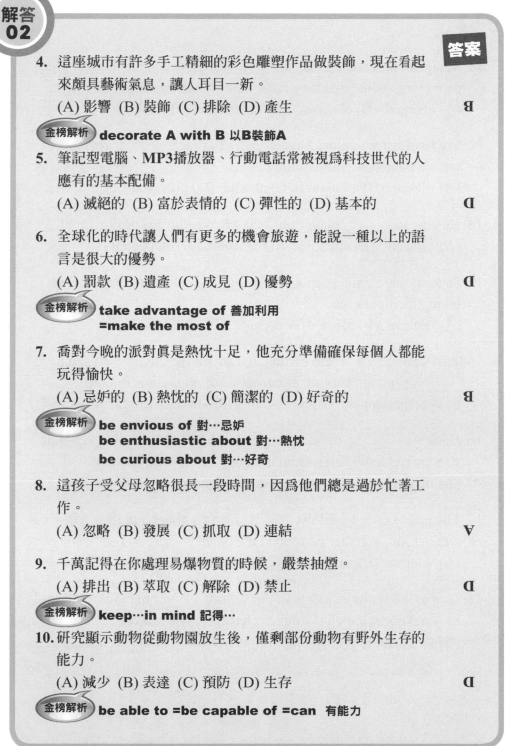

4. 這座城市有許多手工精細的彩色雕塑作品做裝飾，現在看起來頗具藝術氣息，讓人耳目一新。

   (A) 影響 (B) 裝飾 (C) 排除 (D) 產生　　　　　　**B**

   金榜解析 decorate A with B 以B裝飾A

5. 筆記型電腦、MP3播放器、行動電話常被視為科技世代的人應有的基本配備。

   (A) 滅絕的 (B) 富於表情的 (C) 彈性的 (D) 基本的　　**D**

6. 全球化的時代讓人們有更多的機會旅遊，能說一種以上的語言是很大的優勢。

   (A) 罰款 (B) 遺產 (C) 成見 (D) 優勢　　　　　　**D**

   金榜解析 take advantage of 善加利用
   　　　　=make the most of

7. 喬對今晚的派對真是熱忱十足，他充分準備確保每個人都能玩得愉快。

   (A) 忌妒的 (B) 熱忱的 (C) 簡潔的 (D) 好奇的　　**B**

   金榜解析 be envious of 對…忌妒
   　　　　be enthusiastic about 對…熱忱
   　　　　be curious about 對…好奇

8. 這孩子受父母忽略很長一段時間，因為他們總是過於忙著工作。

   (A) 忽略 (B) 發展 (C) 抓取 (D) 連結　　　　　　**A**

9. 千萬記得在你處理易爆物質的時候，嚴禁抽煙。

   (A) 排出 (B) 萃取 (C) 解除 (D) 禁止　　　　　　**D**

   金榜解析 keep…in mind 記得…

10. 研究顯示動物從動物園放生後，僅剩部份動物有野外生存的能力。

   (A) 減少 (B) 表達 (C) 預防 (D) 生存　　　　　　**D**

   金榜解析 be able to =be capable of =can 有能力

11. Many young people today are _____ with fashion and style. They care more about what they wear than what they think or believe.
(A) charged (B) obsessed (C) furnished (D) infected

12. My twin sister's values have _____ so much over the years that we are no longer compatible.
(A) flicked (B) escalated (C) altered (D) deceived

13. He was an _____ player until 20 when he turned professional.
(A) efficient (B) adequate (C) amateur (D) elementary

14. Paparazzi are photographers who _____ celebrities' privacy by taking their pictures.
(A) remove (B) block (C) exclude (D) violate

15. Two years ago a severe earthquake struck the city and caused a _____ tsunami, leaving hundreds dead, thousands injured.
(A) compassionate (B) devastating (C) defensive (D) pessimistic

16. Hank was _____ of accepting bribes because he couldn't explain why he suddenly had so much money in his bank account.
(A) investigated (B) persuaded (C) suspected (D) threatened

17. The police questioned the _____ for two hours, but they still weren't sure whether he robbed the bank.
(A) witness (B) suspect (C) corpse (D) container

18. One of the senior students in our school _____ me today. He said he would beat me up if I didn't give him my sneakers.
(A) threatened (B) opposed (C) elected (D) arrested

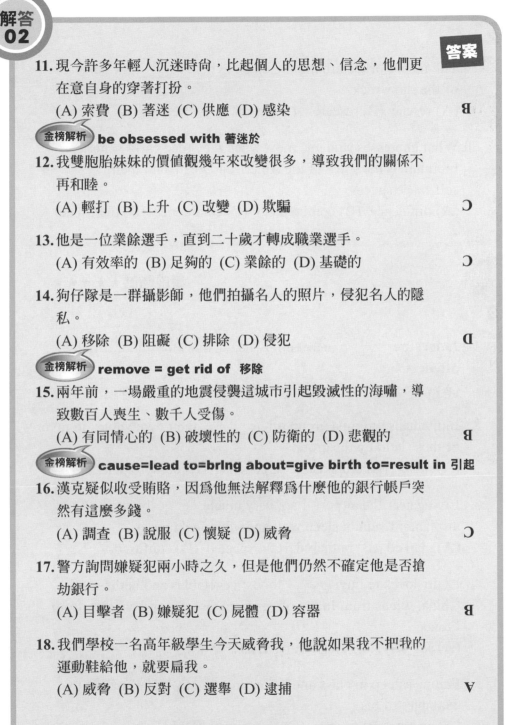

11. 現今許多年輕人沉迷時尚，比起個人的思想、信念，他們更在意自身的穿著打扮。

(A) 索費 (B) 著迷 (C) 供應 (D) 感染　　　　B

金榜解析 be obsessed with 著迷於

12. 我雙胞胎妹妹的價值觀幾年來改變很多，導致我們的關係不再和睦。

(A) 輕打 (B) 上升 (C) 改變 (D) 欺騙　　　　C

13. 他是一位業餘選手，直到二十歲才轉成職業選手。

(A) 有效率的 (B) 足夠的 (C) 業餘的 (D) 基礎的　　　　C

14. 狗仔隊是一群攝影師，他們拍攝名人的照片，侵犯名人的隱私。

(A) 移除 (B) 阻礙 (C) 排除 (D) 侵犯　　　　D

金榜解析 remove = get rid of 移除

15. 兩年前，一場嚴重的地震侵襲這城市引起毀滅性的海嘯，導致數百人喪生、數千人受傷。

(A) 有同情心的 (B) 破壞性的 (C) 防衛的 (D) 悲觀的　　　　B

金榜解析 cause=lead to=bring about=give birth to=result in 引起

16. 漢克疑似收受賄賂，因為他無法解釋為什麼他的銀行帳戶突然有這麼多錢。

(A) 調查 (B) 說服 (C) 懷疑 (D) 威脅　　　　C

17. 警方詢問嫌疑犯兩小時之久，但是他們仍然不確定他是否搶劫銀行。

(A) 目擊者 (B) 嫌疑犯 (C) 屍體 (D) 容器　　　　B

18. 我們學校一名高年級學生今天威脅我，他說如果我不把我的運動鞋給他，就要扁我。

(A) 威脅 (B) 反對 (C) 選舉 (D) 逮捕　　　　A

19. The navy worked around the clock to help _____ the survivors of the shipwreck.
   (A) rescue (B) research (C) retain (D) retreat

20. What impresses students most when they read early American literature is the spirit of the American Dream and their _____ in self-made success.
   (A) diffidence (B) confinement (C) confidence (D) disrespect

考前衝刺★★★★★

1. Judges are _____ increasingly heavy fines for minor driving offences.
   (A) exposing (B) imposing (C) reposing (D) deposing

2. Individuals within a group often _____ their own values in favor of those held by the group.
   (A) prefer (B) emphasize (C) cherish (D) compromise

3. Living near the airport, I am very much _____ by the noise of airplanes. I cannot sleep well and often feel uneasy.
   (A) marked (B) bothered (C) expected (D) confused

4. Claire loves to buy _____ foods: vegetables and herbs from China, spices from India, olives from Greece, and cheeses from France.
   (A) sea (B) stingy (C) tranquil (D) exotic

5. Falling asleep in class and being drowsy at work were just two examples of his _____.
   (A) energy (B) fatigue (C) conspiracy (D) belief

答案

19. 海軍日以繼夜協助搜救船難的生還者。

(A) 搜救 (B) 研究 (C) 保留 (D) 撤退　　　　A

20. 學生在閱讀早期美國文學時,最讓他們印象深刻的,就是美
國夢的精神及白手起家的信心。

(A) 缺乏自信 (B) 限制 (C) 信心 (D) 不敬　　　C

考前衝刺★★★★★

答案

1. 法官對輕微的交通違規現正逐步科以重罰。

(A) 曝露 (B) 對…強加 (C) 使休息 (D) 罷黜　　　B

2. 旅行團成員常常妥協自己的原則以配合旅行團訂下的規則。

(A) 較喜歡 (B) 強調 (C) 珍惜 (D) 妥協　　　D

3. 我住在機場附近,飽受飛機噪音的干擾。我無法好好睡覺,
而且常常感到不安。

(A) 標記 (B) 打擾 (C) 期待 (D) 困惑　　　B

4. 克蕾兒喜愛買異國食物:中國的蔬菜及草藥、印度的香料、
希臘的橄欖與法國的起司。

(A) 海洋 (B) 吝嗇的 (C) 安靜的 (D) 異國的　　　D

5. 他很疲憊,在課堂睡著或是在工作時打瞌睡只是冰山一角。

(A) 能量 (B) 疲憊 (C) 陰謀 (D) 信念　　　B

公職精選歷屆
必考字彙題

6. Elizabeth Anker is a very _____ artist for she is not only an excellent pianist but also a great singer, painter, and poet.
   (A) ethical (B) feeble (C) versatile (D) classical

7. The cake was _____, and tasted bad.
   (A) stale (B) nutritious (C) familiar (D) indispensable

8. To _____ money, buy just what you need and refrain from buying unnecessary stuff.
   (A) invent (B) discard (C) save (D) exhaust

9. With a _____ smile, Robert showed how happy he was when he won the swimming contest yesterday.
   (A) fertile (B) historic (C) pollutant (D) complacent

10. Susan Manning's trip to Buffalo was a/an _____ one. She took her time.
    (A) hasty (B) urgent (C) rapid (D) leisurely

11. Professor Nelson, who is rather strange, displays some _____ behavior from time to time.
    (A) ordinary (B) eccentric (C) comprehensive (D) logical

12. Some families have children in chronic health conditions. At times, the pressure may be _____ to every individual in the family and the challenges can affect the quality of family life.
    (A) encouraging (B) convincing (C) outgoing (D) overwhelming

13. Christopher Reeve was _____ from the neck down and confined to a wheelchair, after the tragic accident.
    (A) paralyzed (B) articulated (C) classified (D) enlightened

答案

6. 伊莉莎白安加是位多才多藝的藝術家，她不僅是一位傑出的
   畫家，同時也是偉大的歌手、畫家、詩人。
   (A) 倫理的 (B) 軟弱的 (C) 多才多藝的 (D) 古典的　　　　C

   金榜解析 not only…but also 不僅…並且

7. 這塊蛋糕發霉了，味道很糟。
   (A) 發霉的 (B) 營養的 (C) 熟悉的 (D) 不可缺少的　　　A

8. 為了省錢，只買你所需的，避免買不需要的東西。
   (A) 發明 (B) 拋棄 (C) 節省 (D) 使耗盡　　　　　　　C

9. 羅伯特昨天贏得游泳比賽時，帶著自滿的微笑，顯得無比快
   樂。
   (A) 肥沃的 (B) 歷史的 (C) 汙染物 (D) 自滿的　　　　D

10. 蘇珊曼寧到水牛城的旅行是一趟悠閒之旅，她玩得很盡興。
    (A) 匆促的 (B) 緊急的 (C) 快速的 (D) 從容不迫的　　　D

    金榜解析 take one's time 從容地…　接動名詞片語
    kill one's time 打發時間…
    waste one's time 浪費時間…
    spend one's time 花費時間…

11. 尼爾森教授相當奇怪，時常做出一些反常的舉動。
    (A) 普通的 (B) 反常的 (C) 廣泛的 (D) 合理的　　　　B

    金榜解析 from time to time=sometimes=at times=occasionally
    =on occasion=once in a while=now and then=every
    now and then 時常

12. 有些家庭的孩子有慢性疾病的狀況。有時候，壓力可能會壓
    倒家中的每一成員，種種挑戰會影響家庭生活品質。
    (A) 給予希望的 (B) 有說服力的 (C) 外向的 (D) 壓倒的　D

13. 克里斯多弗里夫遭逢悲慘的意外之後，頸部以下癱瘓而且行
    動受限於輪椅。
    (A) 使癱瘓 (B) 發音 (C) 分類 (D) 啟發　　　　　　A

公職精選歷屆
必考字彙題

14. Many young Spaniards continued to come to the island, hoping to find gold quickly and become rich _____.
    (A) backward (B) hardly (C) overnight (D) nowhere

15. Since our economy has been improving recently, I hope that my boss will give me a big _____ this year.
    (A) conquest (B) consumption (C) rise (D) raise

16. John Keene's opinion has no _____ on her daughter's decision to become a professional artist. She always gets her own way.
    (A) annoyance (B) revenge (C) record (D) effect

17. The book is about a very _____ boy who always breaks things.
    (A) clumsy (B) appropriate (C) evident (D) fragrant

18. If something is _____, it is dull and depressing.
    (A) measurable (B) dreary (C) graphic (D) hysterical

19. Katherine was reminded to return the book by next Monday, which she _____ from the school library three months ago.
    (A) captured (B) prevented (C) borrowed (D) arrested

20. Sarah, who often attends symphony concerts, has a great _____ for music.
    (A) anxiety (B) disregard (C) appreciation (D) headline

答案

14. 許多年輕的西班牙人相繼來到島上，他們希望趕快發現金礦繼而一夜致富。

(A) 向後地 (B) 幾乎不 (C) 一夜之間 (D) 任何地方都沒有　　C

15. 最近我們的經濟持續在改善，希望老闆今年會給我大幅加薪。

(A) 征服 (B) 消耗 (C) 上升 (D) 加薪　　D

金榜解析 recently=lately=of late　最近地

16. 約翰金尼的看法對女兒毫無影響，她總是堅持自己的路，而決定要成為一位職業藝術家。

(A) 煩擾 (B) 報復 (C) 紀錄 (D) 影響　　D

金榜解析 have no effect on　對…沒有影響

17. 這本書是有關一位非常粗魯的男孩，他總是弄壞東西。

(A) 粗魯的 (B) 適當的 (C) 明顯的 (D) 芳香的　　A

18. 如果某事很枯燥，表示它既單調又令人沮喪。

(A) 可測量的 (B) 令人乏味的 (C) 圖表的 (D) 歇斯底里的　　B

19. 凱薩琳遭點名要在下週一前還書，就是她三個月前向學校圖書館借的那本。

(A) 擄獲 (B) 預防 (C) 借入 (D) 逮捕　　C

20. 莎菈常常參加交響音樂會，她對音樂很有鑑賞力。

(A) 憂鬱 (B) 蔑視 (C) 鑑賞 (D) 頭條新聞　　C

金榜解析 have a great appreciation for　對…頗具鑑賞力

字彙題
04

1. As a result of the accident, Shirley was _____ for three weeks before she gradually recovered.
   (A) unconscious (B) prehistoric (C) gorgeous (D) fortunate

2. For some people, the fear of visiting a _____ outweighs the pain of a toothache.
   (A) barbarian (B) diplomat (C) dentist (D) magician

3. Dr. Morales has confirmed a major _____ in the world of rock art: an ancient rock painting at a burial site from the Inca site of Machu Picchu in Peru.
   (A) epidemic (B) discovery (C) flaw (D) galaxy

4. Some soils are extremely rich in _____ and nutrients such as iron and copper.
   (A) minerals (B) mermaids (C) miniatures (D) manuscripts

5. Scientists have found a _____ for the rare contagious disease, and some patients now have the hope of recovery.
   (A) replacement (B) penalty (C) cure (D) passion

6. Elaine Hadley has many _____, such as horse-back riding, dancing, and playing with animals.
   (A) devices (B) sensations (C) temperaments (D) hobbies

7. People who have a great sense of _____ are often very popular, because they are intelligent, open-minded, and witty.
   (A) frustration (B) humor (C) betrayal (D) inferiority

8. A _____ person is usually welcomed by everyone, because he never irritates people.
   (A) selfish (B) naughty (C) pessimistic (D) humble

答案

1. 由於這場意外事件，雪莉失去知覺長達三星期，之後才逐漸康復。

   (A) 失去知覺的 (B) 史前的 (C) 燦爛的 (D) 幸運的　　　**A**

   金榜解析 as a result of=because of=owing to=on account of 因為

2. 對一些人來說，看牙醫的恐懼勝過牙痛的痛苦。

   (A) 野蠻人 (B) 外交官 (C) 牙醫師 (D) 魔術師　　　**C**

3. 莫瑞里斯博士已經證實岩石藝術界的一項重大發現：來自秘魯瑪丘匹克丘印加遺址墳場的遠古岩石畫作。

   (A) 流行病 (B) 發現 (C) 瑕疵 (D) 銀河系　　　**B**

4. 有些土壤富含礦物質及營養素，例如鐵和銅。

   (A) 礦物質 (B) 美人魚 (C) 縮圖 (D) 原稿　　　**A**

   金榜解析 be rich in 富含…

5. 科學家找到一種罕見傳染病的治療方式，部份病患現在有了治癒的希望。

   (A) 替代 (B) 罰款 (C) 治療 (D) 激情　　　**C**

6. 愛蓮哈德里有許多嗜好，例如騎馬、舞蹈、和動物玩耍等。

   (A) 器具 (B) 知覺 (C) 氣質 (D) 嗜好　　　**D**

7. 有幽默感的人通常很受歡迎，因為他們聰明、心胸開闊又詼諧。

   (A) 挫折 (B) 幽默 (C) 背叛 (D) 劣等　　　**B**

   金榜解析 a sense of humor 幽默感
   a sense of inferiority 自卑感
   a sense of direction 方向感

8. 謙虛的人通常受大家歡迎，因為他從不激怒人。

   (A) 自私的 (B) 頑皮的 (C) 悲觀的 (D) 謙虛的　　　**D**

9. Petroleum production can contribute to air and water pollution; besides, drilling for _____ may disturb the fragile ecosystems.
(A) oil (B) light (C) air (D) truth

10. Kenneth is _____ to confide in others, because he fears that the information he reveals will be used maliciously against him.
(A) happy (B) thankful (C) reluctant (D) voluntary

11. _____ people are sensitive to others' wants and feelings.
(A) Blunt (B) Considerate (C) Arrogant (D) Dominant

12. Ms. Mead has become a media celebrity and an iconic figure who _____ a range of different ideas, values, and beliefs to a broad spectrum of the American public.
(A) alienated (B) buried (C) calculated (D) represented

13. For centuries, artists, historians, and tourists have been _____ by Mona Lisa's enigmatic smile.
(A) ignored (B) characterized (C) fascinated (D) embraced

14. _____ are small, often brightly colored, thin rubber bags that rise and float when they are filled with light gas.
(A) Balloons (B) Flags (C) Peacocks (D) Rainbows

15. As children grow and mature, they will leave behind _____ pursuits, and no longer be so selfish and undisciplined as they used to be.
(A) masculine (B) childish (C) philosophical (D) honorable

16. Dogs usually want to _____ and play with cats, whereas cats are usually afraid and defensive.
(A) chase (B) abandon (C) denounce (D) shun

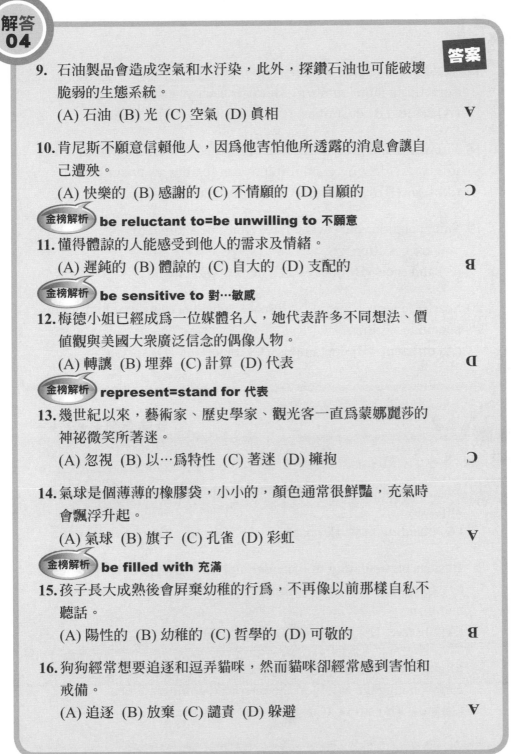

9. 石油製品會造成空氣和水汙染,此外,探鑽石油也可能破壞脆弱的生態系統。

(A) 石油 (B) 光 (C) 空氣 (D) 眞相　　　　A

10. 肯尼斯不願意信賴他人,因爲他害怕他所透露的消息會讓自己遭殃。

(A) 快樂的 (B) 感謝的 (C) 不情願的 (D) 自願的　　C

金榜解析 be reluctant to=be unwilling to 不願意

11. 懂得體諒的人能感受到他人的需求及情緒。

(A) 遲鈍的 (B) 體諒的 (C) 自大的 (D) 支配的　　B

金榜解析 be sensitive to 對…敏感

12. 梅德小姐已經成爲一位媒體名人,她代表許多不同想法、價值觀與美國大衆廣泛信念的偶像人物。

(A) 轉讓 (B) 埋葬 (C) 計算 (D) 代表　　　　D

金榜解析 represent=stand for 代表

13. 幾世紀以來,藝術家、歷史學家、觀光客一直爲蒙娜麗莎的神祕微笑所著迷。

(A) 忽視 (B) 以…爲特性 (C) 著迷 (D) 擁抱　　C

14. 氣球是個薄薄的橡膠袋,小小的,顏色通常很鮮豔,充氣時會飄浮升起。

(A) 氣球 (B) 旗子 (C) 孔雀 (D) 彩虹　　　　A

金榜解析 be filled with 充滿

15. 孩子長大成熟後會屛棄幼稚的行爲,不再像以前那樣自私不聽話。

(A) 陽性的 (B) 幼稚的 (C) 哲學的 (D) 可敬的　　B

16. 狗狗經常想要追逐和逗弄貓咪,然而貓咪卻經常感到害怕和戒備。

(A) 追逐 (B) 放棄 (C) 譴責 (D) 躲避　　　　A

17. Wind and sunshine are very important _____ for Penghu, attracting a large number of tourists each year.
(A) assets (B) quantities (C) propositions (D) materials

18. Fireworks and firecrackers are often used in Chinese communities to _____ greeting good fortunes and scaring away evils.
(A) sign (B) symbolize (C) identify (D) underline

19. Watch out for your own safety! Don't be a target of _____ while you are traveling.
(A) audience (B) thieves (C) heroes (D) clients

20. Scarlet fever is a/an _____ disease, which is transferable from one person to another.
(A) different (B) contagious (C) important (D) special

考前衝刺★★★★★

1. A _____ is a necessary document for the passenger to get on the airplane.
(A) boarding pass (B) passport (C) identification card (D) visa

2. Besides participating in local cultural activities, people who desire to explore the ecology of Kenting can _____ plenty of wildlife and plants.
(A) observe (B) pick up (C) object (D) plan

3. Flight attendants help passengers find their seats and _____ their carry-on luggage safely in the overhead compartments.
(A) stow (B) strew (C) straighten (D) stifle

17. 風和陽光是澎湖非常重要的資產，每年都吸引大批的觀光客。
    (A) 資產 (B) 數量 (C) 提議 (D) 材料 　　　　　　A

18. 煙火和爆竹常用在中國社會，象徵迎接好運及驅趕邪惡。
    (A) 簽名 (B) 象徵 (C) 辨認 (D) 底下畫線 　　　　B

19. 注意你自己的安全！別在旅行時成為小偷的目標。
    (A) 聽眾 (B) 小偷 (C) 英雄 (D) 客戶 　　　　　　B

20. 猩紅熱是一種傳染病，會在人與人之間相互傳染。
    (A) 不同的 (B) 傳染性的 (C) 重要的 (D) 特別的 　　B

答案

考前衝刺★★★★★

答案

1. 登機證是旅客登機所需的證件。
   (A) 登機證 (B) 護照 (C) 身分證 (D) 簽證 　　　　A

2. 除了參與當地文化活動之外，想要探索墾丁生態的人還能觀察大量的野生動植物。
   (A) 觀察 (B) 挑選 (C) 反對 (D) 計畫 　　　　　　A

3. 空服員協助旅客找到座位，並將他們的隨身行李安全裝進座位上方的行李櫃。
   (A) 裝進 (B) 散播 (C) 矯正 (D) 使窒息 　　　　　A

公職精選歷屆
必考字彙題

4. We finished the trip and the cost was well below _____. We had planned to spend three thousand dollars, but we ended up spending only half of that.
   (A) reference (B) reminder (C) budget (D) permission

5. If there is any suspicion of contagious diseases or agricultural pests, the customs agents will impose a _____.
   (A) declaration (B) duty (C) quarantine (D) predicament

6. When people travel to popular destinations during peak seasons, it is necessary to reserve _____ before the trip.
   (A) generation (B) accommodations (C) identification (D) confirmation

7. If you want to find the cheapest airplane ticket, _____ can usually be found through the Internet.
   (A) bargains (B) destinations (C) reservations (D) itinerary

8. Tom's team won the game at the last minute, and the coach was very proud of the _____ of his players.
   (A) performance (B) modulation (C) perception (D) application

9. Don't press the alarm bell unless in absolute _____.
   (A) emergence (B) emergency (C) service (D) status

10. Nowadays, most information has become _____ through the use of computers.
    (A) ordinal (B) fixed (C) available (D) perfect

11. If you have any problems or questions about our new products, you are welcome to use our _____-free service line.
    (A) tax (B) toll (C) money (D) fee

答案

4. 我們的旅行結束了，費用也遠低於預算。我們計畫花費三千元，但最後只花一半而已。
(A) 參考 (B) 提醒者 (C) 預算 (D) 允許   C

5. 如果有任何傳染疾病或農業害蟲的可疑情況，海關人員會強行隔離。
(A) 公告 (B) 責任 (C) 隔離 (D) 危境   C

6. 人們在旅遊旺季到熱門景點旅行時，有必要在行前先預訂住宿。
(A) 世代 (B) 住宿 (C) 辨認 (D) 確認   B

7. 如果你想要找到最便宜的機票，通常可從網站找到。
(A) 廉價品 (B) 目的地 (C) 預定 (D) 旅行指南   A

8. 湯姆的隊伍在最後一分鐘贏得比賽，教練對選手的表現感到非常驕傲。
(A) 表現 (B) 調整 (C) 知覺 (D) 應用   A

9. 除非極度緊急，不然不要觸碰警報鈴。
(A) 發生 (B) 緊急 (C) 服務 (D) 身分   B

10. 目前大部份的訊息已能用電腦取得。
(A) 依序的 (B) 固定的 (C) 可獲得的 (D) 完美的   C

11. 如果您對我們新產品有任何問題或疑問，歡迎使用我們的免付費服務電話。
(A) 稅金 (B) 使用費 (C) 金錢 (D) 費用   B

公職精選歷屆
必考字彙題

12. The amusement park is a famous tourist _____ in Japan. Tourists of all ages love to go there.
(A) attraction (B) fascination (C) information (D) attention

13. Since the president of the company is absent, the general manager will _____ over the meeting.
(A) preview (B) preside (C) pledge (D) persuade

14. Even though you have _____ your flight with the airline, you must still be present at the check-in desk on time.
(A) informed (B) confirmed (C) required (D) given

15. "Don't count your chickens before they are hatched" is a _____ that reminds people not to be too optimistic before their plans succeed.
(A) story (B) proverb (C) history (D) pursuit

16. To increase sales of products, many companies spend huge sums of money on _____ campaigns.
(A) promotion (B) automatic (C) stable (D) solitary

17. Please examine your luggage carefully before leaving. At the security counter, every item in the luggage has to go through thorough _____.
(A) relation (B) invention (C) inspection (D) observation

18. When you are ready to get off an airplane, you will be told not to forget your personal _____.
(A) utilities (B) belongings (C) commodities (D) works

19. Quick and friendly service at the front desk is important to the _____ of tourists.
(A) satisfaction (B) procession (C) procedure (D) prohibition

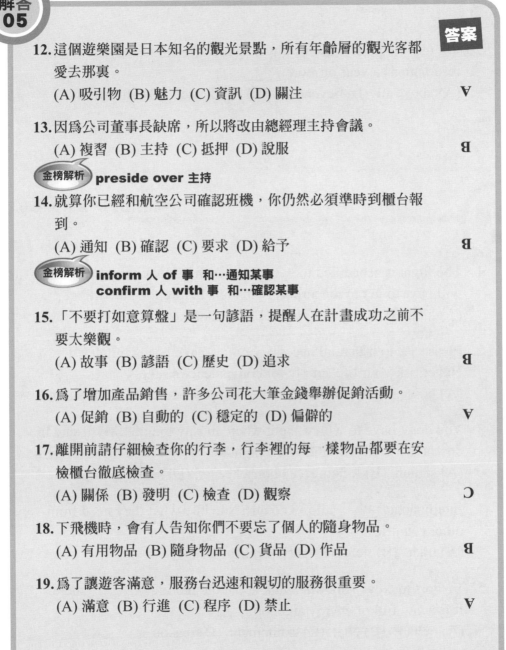

12.這個遊樂園是日本知名的觀光景點，所有年齡層的觀光客都愛去那裏。

(A) 吸引物 (B) 魅力 (C) 資訊 (D) 關注   A

13.因為公司董事長缺席，所以將改由總經理主持會議。

(A) 複習 (B) 主持 (C) 抵押 (D) 說服   B

金榜解析 preside over 主持

14.就算你已經和航空公司確認班機，你仍然必須準時到櫃台報到。

(A) 通知 (B) 確認 (C) 要求 (D) 給予   B

金榜解析 inform 人 of 事　和…通知某事
　　　　confirm 人 with 事　和…確認某事

15.「不要打如意算盤」是一句諺語，提醒人在計畫成功之前不要太樂觀。

(A) 故事 (B) 諺語 (C) 歷史 (D) 追求   B

16.為了增加產品銷售，許多公司花大筆金錢舉辦促銷活動。

(A) 促銷 (B) 自動的 (C) 穩定的 (D) 偏僻的   A

17.離開前請仔細檢查你的行李，行李裡的每　樣物品都要在安檢櫃台徹底檢查。

(A) 關係 (B) 發明 (C) 檢查 (D) 觀察   C

18.下飛機時，會有人告知你們不要忘了個人的隨身物品。

(A) 有用物品 (B) 隨身物品 (C) 貨品 (D) 作品   B

19.為了讓遊客滿意，服務台迅速和親切的服務很重要。

(A) 滿意 (B) 行進 (C) 程序 (D) 禁止   A

20. For tours in peak seasons, travel agents sometimes have to make reservations a year or more _____.
(A) above all (B) beyond all (C) in advance (D) afterwards

考前衝刺★★★★★

1. The flight is scheduled to _____ at eleven o'clock tomorrow. You will have to get to the airport two hours before the takeoff.
(A) land (B) depart (C) cancel (D) examine

2. Please see to it that all necessary _____ have been completed. Never risk your life simply for convenience's sake.
(A) possibilities (B) reservations (C) procedures (D) alternatives

3. You don't have to worry about where to stay tonight. My friend in downtown area will find you a night's _____.
(A) station (B) lodging (C) housekeeper (D) seat

4. International _____ allows countries to buy what they need from other countries.
(A) trade (B) field (C) port (D) trip

5. Visitors to New York often talk about the feeling of _____ there. It is a city full of energy and hope.
(A) culture (B) chat (C) excitement (D) reason

解答 05

20. 爲了因應旅遊旺季，旅行社有時候必須在一年前或更早之前事先預訂。

(A) 尤其 (B) 首要地 (C) 事先地 (D) 之後

答案

C

金榜解析 above all=especially 尤其
in advance=beforehand 事先地

考前衝刺★★★★★

解答 06

答案

1. 班機將於明天十一點起飛，你必須在起飛前兩小時抵達機場。

(A) 降落 (B) 起飛 (C) 取消 (D) 檢查

B

金榜解析 be scheduled to 安排去做…
before the takeoff=before the plane takes off 起飛之前

2. 請留意所有必要程序都已經完成，絕不要貪圖方便而冒生命危險。

(A) 可能性 (B) 預定 (C) 程序 (D) 交替

C

金榜解析 complete the procedures 完成程序
make reservations 預訂

3. 妳不用擔心今晚要住哪裡，我在市中心的朋友會爲妳找到地方暫住一晚。

(A) 車站 (B) 住宿 (C) 家庭主婦 (D) 座位

B

4. 國際貿易允許國與國之間互相購買所需物資。

(A) 貿易 (B) 領域 (C) 港口 (D) 旅行

A

5. 到訪過紐約的人常會談論身處當地的興奮感，那是個充滿活力與希望的城市。

(A) 文化 (B) 聊天 (C) 興奮 (D) 理由

C

公職精選歷屆 必考字彙題

6. In many Western cultures, it is rude to ask about a person's age, weight, or salary. However, these topics may not be as _____ in East Asia.

   (A) economical (B) polluted (C) governed (D) sensitive

7. I enjoy looking at _____ in museums. However, I am too poor to collect any myself.

   (A) websites (B) art pieces (C) crime (D) magazines

8. Cathy is an outgoing and successful salesperson, but her _____ is in web design.

   (A) neighborhood (B) background (C) section (D) system

9. Exploring the culture and history of Africa sounds like a great _____. It will be a lot of fun!

   (A) research (B) abroad (C) adventure (D) space

10. Be sure to dress warmly when _____ in the mountains. It gets cold in the afternoon.

   (A) hiking (B) shopping (C) diving (D) visiting

11. The typhoon that hit southern Taiwan _____ several houses.

   (A) destroyed (B) exhausted (C) increased (D) prevented

12. It's sad that he died of a heart _____.

   (A) attack (B) justice (C) napkin (D) region

13. The new technique in a Malaysia based garment manufacturing company has _____ them to double the production of the factory.

   (A) made (B) enabled (C) persuaded (D) dissuaded

6. 許多西方文化中，詢問他人的年齡、體重或薪資是魯莽的。
   然而在東亞地區，這些話題就不是那麼敏感。
   (A) 節約的 (B) 汙染的 (C) 管制的 (D) 敏感的　　　**D**

7. 我喜愛到博物館觀賞藝術作品。然而，我窮到連一件都收集
   不起。
   (A) 網站 (B) 藝術作品 (C) 犯罪 (D) 雜誌　　　**B**

8. 凱西是一位外向成功的銷售人員，但是她是網站設計出身
   的。
   (A) 鄰近地區 (B) 背景 (C) 部門 (D) 系統　　　**B**

9. 探索非洲的文化歷史聽起來就像一趟偉大的探險，一定會很
   有趣。
   (A) 研究 (B) 海外 (C) 探險 (D) 空間　　　**C**

10. 到山區健行時一定要穿著暖和，每到下午天氣會轉冷。
    (A) 健行 (B) 購物 (C) 潛水 (D) 訪問　　　**A**

11. 侵襲南台灣的颱風損壞當地數棟房子。
    (A) 破壞 (B) 耗盡 (C) 增加 (D) 預防　　　**A**

12. 據說他死於心臟病。
    (A) 攻擊 (B) 公正 (C) 餐巾 (D) 地區　　　**A**

金榜解析 die of 死於疾病
die from 死於受傷或意外

13. 一家馬來西亞的成衣製造公司，其新技術已經讓工廠的生產
    加倍。
    (A) 使 (B) 使能夠 (C) 說服 (D) 勸阻　　　**B**

金榜解析 make + 原形 V.
enable + to + 原形 V.

公職精選歷屆
必考字彙題

14. Many of America's parks and monuments have been made possible by the _____ donations of its citizens.
(A) selfish (B) generous (C) purposeful (D) meaningless

15. The janitor is _____ for taking care of the office.
(A) invited (B) responsible (C) agree (D) good

16. Tom made an _____ to his boss for being late to office.
(A) apologize (B) appreciation (C) apology (D) application

17. There is keen _____ in the sale of mobile phones.
(A) competition (B) explanation (C) discussion (D) compete

18. The post office announces that airmail service to Haiti is temporarily _____ due to the severe earthquake in January.
(A) surprise (B) suspended (C) expense (D) occurred

19. The post office issues _____ stamps for special events only.
(A) commemorative (B) constructive (C) cooperative (D) infinitive

20. I don't think that Tom will have an _____ to get the high-paying job.
(A) chance (B) oath (C) opportunity (D) advice

答案

14. 藉由市民的慷慨捐款，美國許多公園及紀念碑已經有辦法興建。

   (A) 自私的 (B) 慷慨的 (C) 故意的 (D) 無意義的　　　　　B

15. 那位工友負責看管辦公室。

   (A) 邀請 (B) 負責的 (C) 同意 (D) 好的　　　　　B

   金榜解析 be responsible for 負責

16. 湯姆因為上班遲到向老闆道歉。

   (A) 道歉 (B) 欣賞 (C) 道歉 (D) 申請　　　　　C

   金榜解析 make an apology to 人 for 原因
   ＝apologize to 人 for 原因

17. 手機銷售的競爭激烈。

   (A) 競爭 (B) 解釋 (C) 討論 (D) 競爭　　　　　A

   金榜解析 keen competition 激烈的競爭（名詞）
   compete keenly 激烈競爭（動詞）

18. 郵局宣布由於海地一月的嚴重地震，寄往該地的航空郵件暫時停止。

   (A) 驚訝 (B) 停止 (C) 經費 (D) 發生　　　　　B

   金榜解析 be temporarily suspended 暫時停止
   occur 無被動語態

19. 郵局只為特殊事件發行紀念郵票。

   (A) 紀念性的 (B) 建設性的 (C) 合作的 (D) 不定的　　　　　A

20. 我認為湯姆沒有機會獲得高薪的工作。

   (A) 機會 (B) 誓言 (C) 機會 (D) 忠告　　　　　C

   金榜解析 have an opportunity to 得到…的機會

公職精選歷屆
必考字彙題

1. Our hotel provides free ___ service to the airport every day.
   (A) accommodation (B) communication (C) transmission (D) shuttle

2. Rescuers from many countries went to the ___ of the earthquake to help the victims.
   (A) capital (B) refuge (C) epicenter (D) shelter

3. Tourists enjoy visiting night markets around the island to taste ___ local snacks.
   (A) authentic (B) blend (C) inclusive (D) invisible

4. Mike forgot to save the file and the computer ___ suddenly. It was a real disaster.
   (A) broke up (B) was broke (C) was plugged in (D) crashed

5. The ___ at the information desk in a hotel provides traveling information to guests.
   (A) bell hop (B) concierge (C) butler (D) bartender

6. Although the unemployment rate reached an all-time high in mid-2009, it has fallen for four ___ months by December.
   (A) consecutive (B) connecting (C) continual (D) temporary

7. ___ has become a very serious problem in the modern world. It's estimated that there are more than 1 billion overweight adults globally.
   (A) Depression (B) Obesity (C) Malnutrition (D) Starvation

8. Living in a highly ___ society, some Taiwanese children are forced by their parents to learn many skills at a very young age.
   (A) compatible (B) prospective (C) threatened (D) competitive

1. 我們飯店每天提供免費的機場來回接送。
   (A) 住宿 (B) 溝通 (C) 傳輸 (D) 短程來回運輸　　　**D**

2. 來自各國的搜救員前往震央幫助受難者。
   (A) 首都 (B) 庇護 (C) 震央 (D) 避難所　　　**C**

3. 觀光客喜愛到全島各地的夜市品嚐道地小吃。
   (A) 真正的 (B) 混合 (C) 包含的 (D) 看不見的　　　**A**

4. 麥可忘了存檔，結果電腦突然故障，真是一場災難。
   (A) 分手 (B) 故障 (C) 插入插頭 (D) 倒塌　　　**B**

5. 飯店服務台的職員提供旅行資訊給客人。
   (A) 旅館侍者 (B) 服務台職員 (C) 男管家 (D) 酒吧侍者　　　**B**

6. 雖然失業率在二千零九年中期達到高峰，但在十二月之前已
   連續四個月下滑。
   (A) 連續的 (B) 連接的 (C) 不間斷的 (D) 暫時的　　　**A**

7. 肥胖已經成為現代一個嚴重的問題，據估全球有超過十億的
   成人過重。
   (A) 憂鬱 (B) 肥胖 (C) 營養不良 (D) 飢餓　　　B

8. 生活在高度競爭的社會，一些台灣孩子很小的時候就被父母
   逼著去學許多才藝。
   (A) 相容的 (B) 有希望的 (C) 威脅 (D) 競爭的　　　**D**

9. There is clear ___ that the defendant committed the murder of the rich old man.
    (A) research (B) evidence (C) statistics (D) vision

10. The U.S.A. is a _____ country, in which businesses belong mostly to private owners, not to the government.
    (A) capitalist (B) communist (C) socialist (D) journalist

11. John has to ___ the annual report to the manager before this Friday; otherwise, he will be in trouble.
    (A) identify (B) incline (C) submit (D) commemorate

12 Millions of people are expected to ___ in the 2010 Taipei International Flora Expo.
   (A) participate (B) adjust (C) emerge (D) exist

13. It is said that there are only a few lucky days ___ for getting married in 2010.
    (A) elated (B) available (C) elected (D) resentful

14. Tom was ___ from his school for stealing and cheating on the exams.
    (A) exempted (B) expelled (C) exported (D) evacuated

15. Many customers complained that they had difficulty assembling the M-20 mountain bicycle, because the instructions in the manual were not ___.
    (A) implicit (B) explicit (C) complex (D) exquisite

16. There are eight ___ for the Academy Award for the best picture this year.
    (A) attendants (B) nominees (C) conductors (D) producers

答案

9. 有明顯證據指出被告謀殺了那位富有的老先生。

(A) 研究 (B) 證據 (C) 統計學 (D) 視野　　　**B**

10. 美國是個資本主義國家，該國的企業大多是私人擁有，不屬於國家。

(A) 資本主義的 (B) 共產主義者 (C) 社會主義的 (D) 記者　　　**A**

11. 約翰必須在這個星期五之前繳交年度報告給經理，否則他會有麻煩。

(A) 辨認 (B) 使傾向於 (C) 提出 (D) 慶祝　　　**C**

金榜解析 submit…to 向…提出

12. 數百萬人期待參與2010台北國際花卉博覽會。

(A) 參與 (B) 調整 (C) 出現 (D) 生存　　　**A**

金榜解析 participate in 參與

13. 據說二零一零年可以結婚的好日子不多。

(A) 興高采烈的 (B) 可利用的 (C) 選舉的 (D) 不滿的　　　**B**

金榜解析 available for 可用於所修飾的名詞後面

14. 湯姆因為偷竊及考試作弊遭學校開除。

(A) 免除 (B) 開除 (C) 出口 (D) 撤離　　　**B**

金榜解析 be expelled from school 被學校開除

15. 許多顧客抱怨他們組裝M-20越野車時有困難，因為手冊裡的使用說明不明確。

(A) 含蓄的 (B) 明確的 (C) 複雜的 (D) 精緻的　　　**B**

16. 今年奧斯卡金像獎最佳影片共有八部入圍。

(A) 隨從 (B) 提名 (C) 指揮 (D) 製片　　　**B**

公職精選歷屆
必考字彙題

17. Our company has been on a very tight ___ since 2008.
    (A) deficit (B) management (C) budget (D) debt

18. I want to make a/an ___ with Dr. Johnson tomorrow morning. I think I've caught a cold.
    (A) reservation (B) arrangement (C) meeting (D) appointment

19. Diagramming is a method of sentence analysis that uses certain graphic _____ to show the relationship of sentence elements.
    (A) aggressions (B) complications (C) devices (D) heights

20. I love scoring goals in hockey because it _____ gives me a sense of power.
    (A) momentarily (B) monstrously (C) modestly (D) moodily

考前衝刺★★★★★

1. Since the economy is improving, many people are hoping for a ___ in salary in the coming year.
    (A) raise (B) rise (C) surplus (D) bonus

2. I need some ___ for taking buses around town.
    (A) checks (B) exchange (C) change (D) savings

3. Remember to ___ some sunscreen before you go to the beach.
    (A) drink (B) scrub (C) wear (D) move

4. These ancient porcelains are very ___ and might break easily, so please handle them carefully.
    (A) wicked (B) infirm (C) fragile (D) stout

公職精選歷屆
必考字彙題

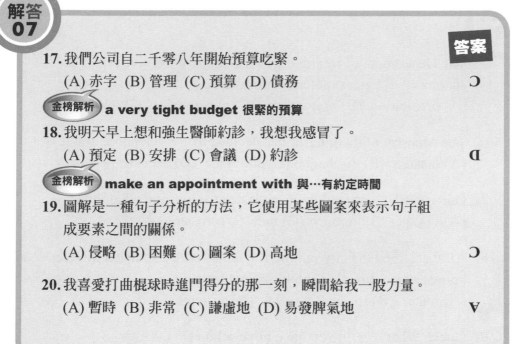

答案

17. 我們公司自二千零八年開始預算吃緊。
    (A) 赤字 (B) 管理 (C) 預算 (D) 債務 　　　　C

    金榜解析 a very tight budget 很緊的預算

18. 我明天早上想和強生醫師約診，我想我感冒了。
    (A) 預定 (B) 安排 (C) 會議 (D) 約診 　　　　D

    金榜解析 make an appointment with 與…有約定時間

19. 圖解是一種句子分析的方法，它使用某些圖案來表示句子組成要素之間的關係。
    (A) 侵略 (B) 困難 (C) 圖案 (D) 高地 　　　　C

20. 我喜愛打曲棍球時進門得分的那一刻，瞬間給我一股力量。
    (A) 暫時 (B) 非常 (C) 謙虛地 (D) 易發脾氣地 　　　　A

考前衝刺★★★★★

答案

1. 經濟持續改善，許多人都希望下一年能加薪。
   (A) 加薪 (B) 上升 (C) 剩餘 (D) 紅利 　　　　A

2. 我需要一些零錢搭公車到鎮上。
   (A) 支票 (B) 匯兌 (C) 零錢 (D) 存款 　　　　C

3. 妳去海灘之前，記得先塗上防曬油。
   (A) 喝 (B) 擦洗 (C) 塗 (D) 搬運 　　　　C

4. 這些古代瓷器非常易碎，可能很容易就會破掉，因此請小心處理。
   (A) 邪惡的 (B) 薄弱的 (C) 易碎的 (D) 堅固的 　　　　C

公職精選歷屆 必考字彙題

5. The Department of Health urged the public to receive H1N1 flu shot as a ___ against potential outbreaks.
   (A) prohibition (B) preparation (C) presumption (D) precaution

6. The Ministry of the Interior has decided to ___ telephone fraud.
   (A) dismiss (B) discharge (C) eliminate (D) execute

7. Our guided ___ around the farm lasted for two and a half hours.
   (A) voyage (B) journey (C) tour (D) crossing

8. All the ___ on the city rail map are color-coded so that a traveler knows which direction she/he should take.
   (A) routes (B) roads (C) sights (D) systems

9. Guest: What ___ do you have in your hotel?
   Hotel clerk: We have a fitness center, a swimming pool, two restaurants, a beauty parlor, and a boutique.
   (A) facilities (B) benefits (C) itineraries (D) details

10. It's difficult to find a hotel with a/an ___ room in high season.
    (A) occupied (B) vacant (C) lank (D) unattended

11. Cathedrals, mosques, and temples are all ___ buildings.
    (A) religious (B) natural (C) political (D) rural

12. If you take a ___ holiday, all your transport, accommodation, and even meals and excursions will be taken care of.
    (A) leisure (B) business (C) package (D) luxury

13. Tourism has helped ___ the economy for many countries, and brought in considerable revenues.
    (A) boast (B) boost (C) receive (D) recall

5. 衛生署呼籲大眾接種**H1N1**流感疫苗注射做爲預防措施，防止爆發的可能性。
   (A) 禁止 (B) 預備 (C) 推測 (D) 預防措施　　**D**

金榜解析 precaution against 對…採取預防措施

6. 內政部決定掃除電話詐騙。
   (A) 使退去 (B) 排出 (C) 消除 (D) 執行　　**C**

7. 我們整個農場的帶隊行程持續了兩個半小時。
   (A) 航程 (B) 旅程 (C) 觀光 (D) 十字路口　　**B**

8. 城市鐵路地圖上的所有路線都是彩色標示，所以旅客可以知道該搭往哪一個方向。
   (A) 路線 (B) 道路 (C) 視力 (D) 系統　　**A**

金榜解析 take…route 向…路線前進

9. 客人：你們飯店有甚麼設施？
   飯店職員：我們有健身中心、游泳池、兩間餐廳、美容院和精品店。
   (A) 設施 (B) 利益 (C) 路線 (D) 細節　　**A**

10. 旺季期間要找到有空房的旅館很困難。
    (A) 占用的 (B) 沒人住的 (C) 細長的 (D) 沒人管的　　**B**

11. 天主教堂、清眞寺及寺廟都是宗教建築。
    (A) 宗教的 (B) 天然的 (C) 政治的 (D) 農村的　　**A**

12. 如果你參加的是跟團旅遊，你所有的交通、住宿、甚至餐飲及行程都會處理好。
    (A) 休閒 (B) 商務 (C) 成套設備 (D) 奢華　　**C**

13. 觀光業有助於促進許多國家的經濟，並帶進可觀的收益。
    (A) 誇耀 (B) 促進 (C) 接受 (D) 回想　　**B**

公職精選歷屆 必考字彙題

14. If you want to work in tourism, you need to know how to work as part of a team. But sometimes, you also need to know how to work ___ .
(A) separately (B) confidently (C) creatively (D) independently

15. Jane completely missed the ___ of what the guest was complaining about.
(A) line (B) goal (C) point (D) plan

16. Many restaurants in Paris offer a ___ of snails for guests to taste.
(A) plate (B) group (C) chunk (D) loaf

17. Slices of lamb are ___ or fried in butter and served with mushrooms, onions, and chips.
(A) added (B) mixed (C) grilled (D) stored

18. The caller: Can I speak to Ms. Taylor in room 612, please?
The operator: Please wait a minute. (pause) I'm sorry. There's no answer. May I ___ a message?
(A) bring (B) take (C) leave (D) send

19. The guest is given a ___ after he makes a complaint to the restaurant.
(A) change (B) profit (C) refund (D) bonus

20. I'm afraid your credit card has already ___ . Would you like to pay in cash instead?
(A) cancelled (B) booked (C) expired (D) exposed

答案

14. 如果你要在旅行業工作，就要知道團隊合作，但有時候你也要知道如何獨立作業。

(A) 分離地 (B) 自信地 (C) 有創意地 (D) 獨立地　　　　**D**

15. 珍完全沒抓到客人抱怨的重點。

(A) 線 (B) 目標 (C) 重點 (D) 計畫　　　　**C**

16. 巴黎許多餐廳會提供一盤蝸牛給客人品嘗。

(A) 一盤 (B) 一組 (C) 一大塊 (D) 一條　　　　**A**

17. 羊肉片火烤或用奶油炸過後，和蘑菇、洋蔥、馬鈴薯片一起上菜。

(A) 加入 (B) 混合 (C) 烤 (D) 儲存　　　　**C**

18. 來電者：麻煩請六一二室的泰勒女士接電話。

總機：請稍候。抱歉，無人回應。我能為您留言嗎？

(A) 帶來 (B) 寫下 (C) 留下 (D) 寄送　　　　**B**

> **金榜解析** take a message 為人留言
> leave a message 當事人留言

19. 那位客人向餐廳抱怨之後得到一筆退款。

(A) 零錢 (B) 利益 (C) 退款 (D) 紅利　　　　**C**

20. 你的信用卡恐怕已經到期，可以麻煩您改成付現嗎？

(A) 取消 (B) 訂票 (C) 到期 (D) 曝露　　　　**C**

公職精選歷屆 **必考**字彙題

字彙題 09

1. You and your partner are_____ if you share similar life goals and can work together toward them.
   (A) comparative (B) compatible (C) compelling (D) complicit

2. The restaurant is one of the few_____ for dance parties in the area.
   (A) venues (B) ventures (C) revenues (D) vendors

3. Whenever a new incinerator is proposed to build, people hold a _____ protesting against building it in their neighborhood.
   (A) celebration (B) demonstration (C) display (D) parade

4. There seemed to be a _____ agreement between the two fighting countries that neither side would fire on Christmas Eve.
   (A) messy (B) plummeting (C) cascading (D) tacit

5. Scientists have recently found that the future cancer _____ will not depend on where the cancer started but which gene is damaged.
   (A) symptom (B) recipe (C) syndromes (D) therapy

6. After a three-day strike, the employer and the employees have reached a consensus, and the factory has _____ operations.
   (A) reflected (B) resumed (C) represented (D) offered

7. The production of rice and wheat in this country is _____ by the local government.
   (A) giving (B) subject (C) subsidized (D) grow

8. The river was _____ by the chemical waste from the factory.
   (A) contained (B) crossed (C) collected (D) contaminated

解答 09

答案

1. 如果你和你的夥伴有相同的生活目標，且能共同朝這些目標努力，你們就能和睦相處。
   (A) 比較的 (B) 共處的 (C) 可強迫的 (D) 同謀的　　　**B**

2. 這家餐廳是該區少數可以辦舞會的地點之一。
   (A) 地點 (B) 冒險 (C) 收益 (D) 攤販　　　**A**

3. 每當提議興建焚化爐時，人們就會示威抗議興建在他們的鄰近地區。
   (A) 慶祝 (B) 示威 (C) 展現 (D) 遊行　　　**B**

4. 這兩個交戰國之間似乎有一個心照不宣的協議，就是任一方都不會在聖誕夜開火。
   (A) 凌亂的 (B) 跌落的 (C) 串聯的 (D) 不明言的　　　**D**

5. 科學家已經發現未來癌症的治療將不會視腫瘤在哪個部位發病而定，而是要看哪一個基因受損。
   (A) 徵兆 (B) 處方 (C) 症候群 (D) 療法　　　**D**

6. 罷工三天之後，僱主和員工達成共識，工廠也已經恢復運作。
   (A) 反射 (B) 恢復 (C) 代表 (D) 提供　　　**B**

7. 這國家的稻米及小麥的生產是由地方政府補助。
   (A) 給予 (B) 受支配的 (C) 補助 (D) 種植　　　**C**

   金榜解析 be+過去分詞+by，過去分詞表示被動語態

8. 這條河流遭工廠的化學廢料汙染。
   (A) 包含 (B) 跨越 (C) 收集 (D) 汙染　　　**D**

公職精選歷屆 **必考**字彙題

9. You have the _____ of going to work or studying abroad.
   (A) alternatives (B) changes (C) alterations (D) character

10. The food here is _____ but water is running short.
    (A) plentiful (B) lacking (C) consistent (D) scarce

11. Cosmetic surgery is now _____ throughout Asia. In Thailand, a million procedures were performed in 2000, doubled the number from five years ago.
    (A) booming (B) intruding (C) mourning (D) plunging

12. In Taipei you can buy a huge _____ of ready-to-eat food at street stalls or in shops, to take out and eat as you walk along.
    (A) chunk (B) variety (C) package (D) satchel

13. The products of Taiwan's small-scale agriculture have suffered severely both in _____ and overseas markets.
    (A) domestic (B) essential (C) sufficient (D) voluntary

14. With the intense heat, the chocolate bar began to melt and thus became _____.
    (A) sunk (B) sticky (C) lengthy (D) remaining

15. The founder of the company, born into the family living below poverty line, built his corporate empire from _____.
    (A) sketch (B) scandal (C) script (D) scratch

16. The teacher showed great concern about Steven's _____ at school because he had missed five days of classes last month.
    (A) consequence (B) significance (C) dependence (D) attendance

答案

9. 你可以選擇去工作或出國念書。
   (A) 選擇 (B) 改變 (C) 變化 (D) 角色　　　　　A

10. 這裡的食物豐富，但是水源漸漸不足。
    (A) 豐富的 (B) 缺乏的 (C) 一致的 (D) 罕見的　　　A

11. 整形手術目前在全亞洲蓬勃發展。泰國在二千年時有一百萬件，是五年前的一倍之多。
    (A) 趨於興隆 (B) 侵入 (C) 悲傷 (D) 插入　　　A

12. 在台北，你可以在路邊攤或商店外帶各式各樣的熟食，然後邊走邊吃。
    (A) 大塊 (B) 多樣化 (C) 包裹 (D) 小背包　　　B

金榜解析 a variety of 各式各樣的

13. 台灣小規模農產品在國內與國外市場皆受重創。
    (A) 國內的 (B) 基本的 (C) 足夠的 (D) 自願的　　　A

14. 巧克力棒因為太熱而開始融化，變得黏黏的。
    (A) 灰心的 (B) 黏的 (C) 冗長的 (D) 殘留　　　B

15. 公司創辦人出生赤貧家庭，他白手起家建立自己的企業王國。
    (A) 草稿 (B) 醜聞 (C) 手跡 (D) 起跑點　　　D

金榜解析 from scratch 白手起家

16. 老師高度關切史提芬出席狀況，因為他上個月已經缺席了五天的課程。
    (A) 後果 (B) 意義 (C) 依賴 (D) 出席　　　D

公職精選歷屆 **必考**字彙題

17. Leaders of the world's biggest economies sought on Saturday to settle their remaining differences over an emergency plan to counter the worst financial _____ in decades.
(A) cricket (B) cripple (C) critic (D) crisis

18. In Turkey, many people are _____. You're supposed to smile when you see the new moon in the sky. The moon will bring good fortune if you do so.
(A) superficial (B) superior (C) superb (D) superstitious

19. Taiwan stocks closed higher despite _____ in U.S. stocks in overnight trading, as analysts expressed optimism for local shares in the short run.
(A) bailout (B) decline (C) inflation (D) recovery

20. The job market is getting more and more _____ because of the high unemployment rate.
(A) competitive (B) influential (C) measurable (D) professional

考前衝刺★★★★★

1. All the movie fans are looking forward to the _____ of the director's latest film.
(A) competition (B) marathon (C) premiere (D) evolution

2. _____ is now the new norm in the world of business so that any projection almost seems redundant.
(A) Versatility (B) Ventilation (C) Vehement (D) Volatility

答案

17. 世界最大經濟體的各國領袖於周六試圖解決一項緊急計劃中彼此所殘存的歧見，該計畫希望能夠對抗數十年來最嚴重的金融危機。

(A) 蟋蟀 (B) 殘廢者 (C) 批評 (D) 危機　　　**D**

金榜解析 seek to 尋求；試圖

18. 在土耳其，多數人都很迷信。看見天空的新月時，應該要笑，如此一來，月亮將會帶給你好運。

(A) 膚淺的 (B) 優越的 (C) 超級的 (D) 迷信的　　　**D**

19. 儘管美股一夜交易後下跌，但分析師對台灣當地股票短線看法樂觀，因此台股仍高點收盤。

(A) 應付緊急狀況的 (B) 衰退 (C) 通貨膨脹 (D) 恢復　　　**B**

20. 因為高失業率，職業市場變得越來越競爭。

(A) 競爭的 (B) 有影響力的 (C) 可測量的 (D) 專業的　　　**A**

考前衝刺★★★★★

答案

1. 所有影迷都期待那位導演最新的電影首映。
(A) 競爭 (B) 馬拉松 (C) 首映 (D) 進化　　　**C**

2. 瞬息萬變是目前商界的新準則，因此任何推測似乎都是多餘的。
(A) 全面性 (B) 通風 (C) 激烈的 (D) 易變　　　**D**

公職精選歷屆 **必考**字彙題

3. To comply with the government _____ regulations, we are required to order from the accredited sellers.
(A) jurisdiction (B) execution (C) procurement (D) quotations

4. The idea that the research team could have fudged the result was as _____ as it was offensive.
(A) prosperous (B) preposterous (C) prospective (D) prescriptive

5. The manufacturer offered unlimited _____ on all their products to expand the market.
(A) warranty (B) securities (C) subsidiary (D) authorization

6. Many banks have chipped away at the mountain of mortgages and credit card debt _____ over struggling consumers.
(A) roaming (B) moonlighting (C) savoring (D) looming

7. In its dot-com _____, Silicon Valley was practically minting millionaires every day.
(A) burst (B) heyday (C) duel (D) footfall

8. It is generally agreed that trendy high-tech _____ are most appealing to younger population.
(A) ghettos (B) emblem (C) gizmos (D) emerald

9. If you are nervous, you can take a deep _____ to calm down.
(A) breath (B) client (C) flame (D) grain

10. "Sex and the City" and "Friends" were very famous _____ in Taiwan.
(A) sitcoms (B) profiles (C) institutes (D) inventories

3. 爲了符合政府採購規定，我們必須向合格廠商訂購。
   (A) 司法權 (B) 執行 (C) 採購 (D) 估價　　　　　　C

4. 若認爲研究團隊會去捏造結果，這想法簡直是又荒謬又無禮。
   (A) 繁榮的 (B) 荒謬的 (C) 預期的 (D) 規定的　　　　B

5. 製造商提供所有產品無限責任擔保來擴張市場。
   (A) 保證 (B) 安全 (C) 附屬品 (D) 權威　　　　　　A

6. 生計維艱的客戶受大量貸款和卡債的逼迫，許多銀行將此情況慢慢縮小。
   (A) 漫遊 (B) 打工 (C) 使有氣味 (D) 逼近　　　　　D

   金榜解析 loom over 緩緩接近；逼近

7. 在網路商業全盛時期，矽谷幾乎每天都會創造出百萬富翁。
   (A) 爆發 (B) 全盛期 (C) 競爭 (D) 橄欖球　　　　　B

8. 一般都認同時髦的高科技小發明最能吸引年輕族群。
   (A) 少數民族聚集區 (B) 徽章 (C) 小發明 (D) 綠寶石　C

9. 你如果緊張的話，可以深呼吸讓自己平靜。
   (A) 呼吸 (B) 客戶 (C) 火焰 (D) 穀物　　　　　　A

   金榜解析 take a deep breath 深呼吸

10. 「慾望城市」及「六人行」是曾在台灣紅極一時的情景喜劇。
    (A) 情景喜劇 (B) 人物簡介 (C) 學院 (D) 財產清單　A

公職精選歷屆
必考字彙題

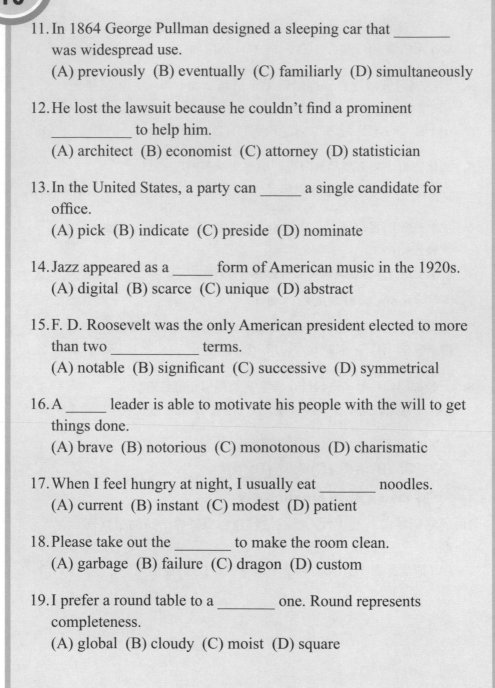

11. In 1864 George Pullman designed a sleeping car that _____ was widespread use.
(A) previously (B) eventually (C) familiarly (D) simultaneously

12. He lost the lawsuit because he couldn't find a prominent _____ to help him.
(A) architect (B) economist (C) attorney (D) statistician

13. In the United States, a party can _____ a single candidate for office.
(A) pick (B) indicate (C) preside (D) nominate

14. Jazz appeared as a _____ form of American music in the 1920s.
(A) digital (B) scarce (C) unique (D) abstract

15. F. D. Roosevelt was the only American president elected to more than two _____ terms.
(A) notable (B) significant (C) successive (D) symmetrical

16. A _____ leader is able to motivate his people with the will to get things done.
(A) brave (B) notorious (C) monotonous (D) charismatic

17. When I feel hungry at night, I usually eat _____ noodles.
(A) current (B) instant (C) modest (D) patient

18. Please take out the _____ to make the room clean.
(A) garbage (B) failure (C) dragon (D) custom

19. I prefer a round table to a _____ one. Round represents completeness.
(A) global (B) cloudy (C) moist (D) square

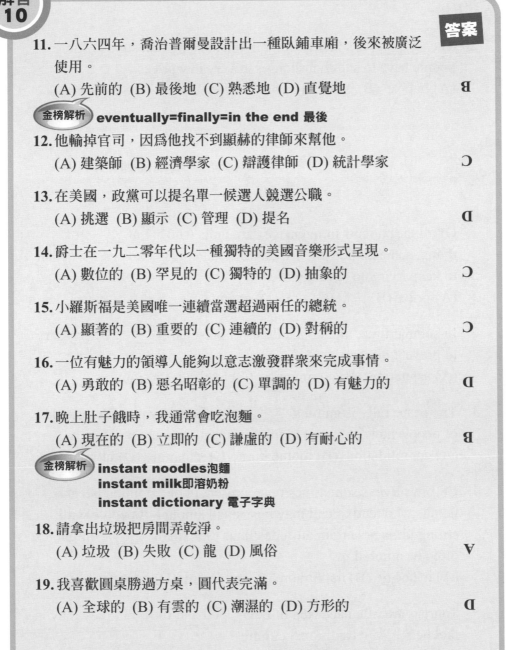

答案

11. 一八六四年，喬治普爾曼設計出一種臥鋪車廂，後來被廣泛使用。

(A) 先前的 (B) 最後地 (C) 熟悉地 (D) 直覺地 　　B

金榜解析 eventually=finally=in the end 最後

12. 他輸掉官司，因為他找不到顯赫的律師來幫他。

(A) 建築師 (B) 經濟學家 (C) 辯護律師 (D) 統計學家 　　C

13. 在美國，政黨可以提名單一候選人競選公職。

(A) 挑選 (B) 顯示 (C) 管理 (D) 提名 　　D

14. 爵士在一九二零年代以一種獨特的美國音樂形式呈現。

(A) 數位的 (B) 罕見的 (C) 獨特的 (D) 抽象的 　　C

15. 小羅斯福是美國唯一連續當選超過兩任的總統。

(A) 顯著的 (B) 重要的 (C) 連續的 (D) 對稱的 　　C

16. 一位有魅力的領導人能夠以意志激發群眾來完成事情。

(A) 勇敢的 (B) 惡名昭彰的 (C) 單調的 (D) 有魅力的 　　D

17. 晚上肚子餓時，我通常會吃泡麵。

(A) 現在的 (B) 立即的 (C) 謙虛的 (D) 有耐心的 　　B

金榜解析 instant noodles泡麵
instant milk即溶奶粉
instant dictionary 電子字典

18. 請拿出垃圾把房間弄乾淨。

(A) 垃圾 (B) 失敗 (C) 龍 (D) 風俗 　　A

19. 我喜歡圓桌勝過方桌，圓代表完滿。

(A) 全球的 (B) 有雲的 (C) 潮濕的 (D) 方形的 　　D

公職精選歷屆 必考字彙題

20. The _____ has finally burst in the housing industry, so some people have to sell their houses at very low prices.
(A) bubble (B) gallon (C) hammer (D) kitten

考前衝刺★★★★★

1. Of all the patients in intensive care units who are at _____ of dying, some 20 percent present difficult ethical choices—whether to keep trying to save the life.
(A) price (B) risk (C) rim (D) attempt

2. In summertime, higher standards of personal _____ are necessary to prevent disease.
(A) aspiration (B) commodity (C) hygiene (D) routine

3. The peace rally is gaining _____ every hour. By now, thousands of people have gathered in front of the parliament building.
(A) consolidation (B) momentum (C) radiation (D) ultimatum

4. Call-in surveys sometimes misrepresent public opinion because people who tend to call may be a small amount of people with strong ideas or certain attitudes; thus the "silent _____" might often be ignored.
(A) majority (B) maximum (C) minimum (D) minority

5. Tourists are often accused of being loud and rude, but they may in fact help _____ traditional cultures.
(A) abuse (B) impede (C) hinder (D) sustain

答案

20. 房市最後泡沫化了，因此有些人必須以非常低的價格賣掉他
們的房子。
(A) 泡沫 (B) 加侖 (C) 榔頭 (D) 小貓   A

考前衝刺★★★★★

解答
11

答案

1. 加護病房裡生命垂危的病人中，百分之二十左右的人面臨道
德抉擇的難題，那就是該不該繼續搶救生命。
(A) 價錢 (B) 冒險 (C) 邊緣 (D) 企圖   B

金榜解析 at risk 處於危險

2. 夏季需要較高的個人衛生標準來預防疾病。
(A) 呼吸 (B) 日用品 (C) 衛生 (D) 例行公事   C

3. 和平集會每小時都不斷在增強氣勢，截至目前為止已有數千
人聚集在國會大樓前。
(A) 鞏固 (B) 推動力 (C) 發光 (D) 最後通牒   B

4. 叩應調查有時候會曲解公共意見，因為會想打電話的人可能
是那些帶著強烈意見或特定態度的少數，「沉默的多數」因
此常被忽略。
(A) 大多數 (B) 最大限度 (C) 最少限度 (D) 少數   A

5. 觀光客常因大聲及魯莽遭指責，但事實上他們可能有助於維
護傳統文化。
(A) 濫用 (B) 阻礙 (C) 妨礙 (D) 維護   D

金榜解析 be accused of 因…遭指責

公職精選歷屆
必考字彙題

6. It is an excellent plan on paper, but from a practical point of view, it just isn't _____.
   (A) feasible (B) visible (C) gullible (D) vulnerable

7. These companies claim deeper seawater contains more _____ and fewer pollutants than surface water.
   (A) cankers (B) nutrients (C) incentives (D) utilities

8. At the airport, the customs officials usually open our bags to _____ the contents.
   (A) expect (B) retrospect (C) prospect (D) inspect

9. Being surrounded by the strong force of the police, the gangsters couldn't but _____ .
   (A) defeat (B) regulate (C) surrender (D) tolerate

10. The _____ woman made a point of visiting people in the hospital who had no relatives to visit them.
    (A) benevolent (B) ruthless (C) ceremonial (D) supreme

11. The government brutally _____ the students' protest, which in turn stimulated violent backlash.
    (A) collided (B) rebelled (C) alienated (D) suppressed

12. The actress was considered a new star in the film industry. Her first performance caused quite a _____ .
    (A) symptom (B) substance (C) sensation (D) shortage

13. Although the leader sometimes tends to _____ the situation, the team works well together.
    (A) dominate (B) combine (C) invest (D) accumulate

答案

6. 理論上這是一個很棒的計畫，但是從務實觀點來看，並不可行。

(A) 可實行的 (B) 看得見的 (C) 易上當的 (D) 易受攻擊的　　A

7. 這些公司宣稱深層水比表層水包含更多的營養物及較少的汙染物。

(A) 弊端 (B) 營養物 (C) 誘因 (D) 公用事業　　B

8. 在機場，海關人員經常會打開袋子檢查裡面的東西。

(A) 期待 (B) 追憶 (C) 探測 (D) 檢查　　D

9. 幫派份子遭警方強大火力包圍而不得不投降。

(A) 打敗 (B) 調整 (C) 投降 (D) 容忍　　C

金榜解析 不得不的兩種句型：could not but+原形動詞
could not help+動名詞

10. 那位慈善的婦人堅持要去醫院探視那些沒有親人探訪的人。

(A) 慈善的 (B) 殘忍的 (C) 講究儀式的 (D) 至高的　　A

金榜解析 make a point of =insist upon 堅持

11. 政府粗暴鎮壓學生的抗議行動，此舉反而引發更激烈的反擊。

(A) 撞擊 (B) 背叛 (C) 疏遠 (D) 鎮壓　　D

12. 這位女演員被認為是電影業的一顆新星。她首次演出就造成相當的轟動。

(A) 症狀 (B) 物質 (C) 轟動 (D) 缺乏　　C

13. 雖然領導者有時意圖主導情勢，但團隊通力合作結果才會好。

(A) 主導 (B) 結合 (C) 投資 (D) 累積　　A

公職精選歷屆
必考字彙題

14. Fortunately, the patient's condition remains _____ after the operation. She will be recovering soon.
(A) critical (B) vulnerable (C) radical (D) stable

15. My bookshelves were destroyed in the flood. I need to find a _____ to fix them.
(A) burglar (B) carpenter (C) plumber (D) physician

16. Visitors to the museum have to _____ an entrance fee.
(A) buy (B) fine (C) pay (D) fix

17. This has been a long discussion. I hope we can come to some _____ by dinner time.
(A) agreement (B) battle (C) meaning (D) purpose

18. He is very _____ . He always looks on the bright side of life.
(A) pessimistic (B) optimistic (C) imaginary (D) inventive

19. The corporation can offer more opportunities to the efficient and _____ employees and thus secure top-flight personnel.
(A) ambitious (B) anxious (C) ambivalent (D) ambiguous

20. Unfortunately, the hotel is extremely limited in space and cannot _____ large groups of tourists.
(A) accommodate (B) anticipate (C) inhabit (D) dwell

14. 幸好病人的術後狀況穩定，她很快就會復原。
(A) 批評的 (B) 脆弱的 (C) 基本的 (D) 穩定的 　　D

15. 我的書櫃在淹水時受損，我需要找一位木匠來修理。
(A) 夜賊 (B) 木匠 (C) 水管工人 (D) 醫生 　　B

16. 參觀博物館的遊客必須付入場費。
(A) 買 (B) 罰款 (C) 付錢 (D) 修理 　　C

17. 這事已經討論很久了，我希望我們能夠在晚餐前達成協議。
(A) 協議 (B) 戰役 (C) 意義 (D) 目的 　　A

金榜解析 come to agreement 達成協議
under discussion 討論中

18. 他非常樂觀，總是看待生命的光明面。
(A) 悲觀的 (B) 樂觀的 (C) 虛構的 (D) 有發明才智的 　　B

19. 公司會提供更多機會給有能力和企圖心強的員工，因此能夠
保障第一流的人員。
(A) 有抱負的 (B) 焦慮的 (C) 有矛盾感情的 (D) 分歧的 　　A

20. 不幸的是這家旅館空間極為有限，無法容納人數龐大的旅行
團。
(A) 容納 (B) 預期 (C) 棲息 (D) 居住 　　A

字彙題 12

1. I am sure I had made quite a good _____ on the personnel manager in the interview because I got the job.
   (A) interpretation (B) expression (C) transition (D) impression

2. Strong social skills can enhance a child's _____ , emotional and physical development.
   (A) empirical (B) impressive (C) cognitive (D) virtual

3. The teacher thought the question was difficult but the student came to the answer in a _____ .
   (A) blow (B) break (C) flex (D) flash

4. Confucianism _____ Chinese life and culture for over two thousand years.
   (A) perforated (B) permeated (C) perpetuated (D) perplexed

5. It was a great _____ for Helen to find her husband and children survived the car accident.
   (A) relax (B) release (C) relief (D) relieve

6. The mayor determined to build a _____ city. By then, users can get access to the Internet at any time and any place in the city.
   (A) commuter (B) digital (C) electric (D) remote

7. Jack _____ to help clean the classroom after school. Everybody is surprised because he is usually very lazy.
   (A) forgets (B) refuses (C) declines (D) volunteers

8. Cheating in exams is a serious _____ of the school regulations.
   (A) crime (B) violation (C) destruction (D) rejection

9. The convicted man _____ against the judge's verdict because new evidence had proved his innocence.
   (A) appalled (B) appeased (C) appealed (D) appeared

解答
12

答案

1. 我相信我在面談中給人事經理留下很好的印象,因為我獲得了這份工作。
   (A) 解釋 (B) 表達 (C) 變化 (D) 印象　　**D**

   金榜解析 make a good impression on 給…留下好印象

2. 高超的社交技巧能增強小孩子在認知、情緒及體能上的發展。
   (A) 憑經驗的 (B) 感人的 (C) 認知的 (D) 實質的　　**C**

3. 老師認為問題很困難,但是學生一下子就找到答案。
   (A) 吹 (B) 休息 (C) 電線 (D) 一瞬間　　**D**

   金榜解析 in a flash 一瞬間

4. 儒家思想遍及中國人的生活與文化兩千多年。
   (A) 穿孔 (B) 遍及 (C) 使永恆 (D) 使複雜　　**B**

5. 海倫得知她丈夫和孩子在車禍中生還,感到如釋重負。
   (A) 放鬆 (B) 解開 (C) 釋然 (D) 緩和　　**C**

6. 市長決定建造一座數位城市。到那時,使用者就能在市區隨時隨地上網。
   (A) 通勤者 (B) 數位的 (C) 電子的 (D) 遙遠的　　**B**

7. 傑克放學後自願幫忙清理教室讓每個人都很驚訝,因為他平常很懶惰。
   (A) 忘記 (B) 拒絕 (C) 婉謝 (D) 自願　　**D**

8. 考試作弊嚴重違反校規。
   (A) 犯罪 (B) 違規 (C) 破壞 (D) 拒絕　　**B**

9. 犯人對法官的判決提出上訴,因為新證據已證明他無罪。
   (A) 使恐懼 (B) 調停 (C) 上訴 (D) 呈現　　**C**

   金榜解析 appeal against 上訴

10. _____ help us fly kites in spring and cool us in summer.
(A) Typhoons (B) Storms (C) Hurricanes (D) Breezes

11. The government hopes that the charge for trash disposal can
_____ people from throwing away usable resources.
(A) interrupt (B) persuade (C) force (D) discourage

12. Tammy receives no payment because she is a _____ worker in the
hospital. She works there just because she enjoys helping people.
(A) skeptical (B) permanent (C) volunteer (D) mandatory

13. Tom comes from a wealthy family, but John does not. In spite of
their different _____, they have become best friends.
(A) backgrounds (B) interests (C) personalities (D) habits

14. The pianist's performance of Franz Liszt's piano pieces was an
_____ of skill and strength.
(A) expectation (B) abbreviation (C) irritation (D) exhibition

15. The power supply in this area is not _____ . You had better save
your file every ten minutes.
(A) available (B) probable (C) stable (D) capable

16. Any revision of the law should be _____ with the overall goal of
the government's policy. The priority should be placed on the
welfare of the citizens.
(A) sensible (B) consonant (C) significant (D) remarkable

17. The government is figuring out ways to maintain our economic
_____ so that the unemployment rate will go down.
(A) recession (B) mentality (C) depression (D) vitality

10. 微風能讓我們在春天放風箏，並在夏天時使我們涼快。

(A) 颱風 (B) 暴風雨 (C) 颶風 (D) 微風 　　　　　　　**D**

11. 政府希望收取垃圾處理費能夠打消民眾丟棄可用資源的念頭。

(A) 打斷 (B) 說服 (C) 強迫 (D) 勸阻 　　　　　　　**D**

12. 泰咪是醫院的志工所以不受薪，她在那裏工作僅是因爲樂於助人。

(A) 多疑的 (B) 耐久的 (C) 自願的 (D) 委託的 　　　　　　　**C**

13. 湯姆來自富裕的家庭，但約翰不是。儘管家庭背景不同，他們仍然成爲最好的朋友。

(A) 背景 (B) 興趣 (C) 人格 (D) 習慣 　　　　　　　**A**

14. 那位鋼琴家演奏弗朗茨李斯特的鋼琴作品是一種技巧和力量的展現。

(A) 期待 (B) 縮寫 (C) 激怒 (D) 展現 　　　　　　　**D**

15. 這區的電力供應不穩定，你最好每十分鐘存一次檔案。

(A) 可獲得的 (B) 可能的 (C) 穩定的 (D) 有能力的 　　　　　　　**C**

16. 任何法律修訂都應與政府政策的整體目標一致，並以公民福祉爲優先。

(A) 可感覺的 (B) 一致的 (C) 顯著的 (D) 引人注目的 　　　　　　　**B**

金榜解析 be consonant with 與…一致

17. 政府正想辦法要維持經濟活絡，好降低失業率。

(A) 不景氣 (B) 心理狀態 (C) 蕭條 (D) 活力 　　　　　　　**D**

18. Paul was charged with _____ driving after he was arrested for running over an old man.
(A) reckless (B) relaxed (C) safe (D) solemn

19. Tim _____ down 12 cans of beer in 10 minutes and didn't show any sign of being drunk.
(A) broke (B) drizzled (C) gulped (D) sipped

20. Since being slim is the trend, Margaret is trying to lose weight by _____ herself.
(A) starving (B) amusing (C) nourishing (D) inventing

考前衝刺★★★★★

字彙題
13

1. When the pop idol came to Taiwan, swarms of fans crowded the street outside the hotel, waiting for a _____ of their hero.
(A) catch (B) glimpse (C) grasp (D) thought

2. I usually buy daily necessities in the same grocery store. The clerks know me because I'm a regular _____ .
(A) patient (B) owner (C) customer (D) entertainer

3. Being an assistant is just a _____ job. Allen plans to find a permanent position in an international corporation.
(A) gradual (B) previous (C) suitable (D) temporary

4. Acid rain causes the ground to release _____ substances; plants and trees are thus slowly poisoned.
(A) barren (B) gross (C) toxic (D) weary

公職精選歷屆
必考字彙題

答案

18. 保羅撞倒一位老先生，他被補後以過失駕駛遭起訴。

(A) 魯莽的　(B) 鬆懈的　(C) 安全的　(D) 嚴肅的　　V

金榜解析 be charged with 被起訴

19. 提姆十分鐘內喝下十二罐啤酒，但毫無酒醉的跡象。

(A) 打破　(B) 下毛毛雨　(C) 吞飲　(D) 啜飲　　C

20. 有鑑於苗條是種趨勢，瑪格瑞特想要靠挨餓來減肥。

(A) 使挨餓　(B) 使歡樂　(C) 施肥　(D) 發明　　V

考前衝刺★★★★★

答案

1. 那位人氣正夯的偶像來台灣時，成群的粉絲擠爆飯店外的街
   道等著一窺他們的英雄。
   (A) 捕抓　(B) 瞥見　(C) 緊握　(D) 想法　　B

2. 我經常在同一家雜貨店買日常用品，我是常客店員都認識
   我。
   (A) 病人　(B) 擁有者　(C) 顧客　(D) 藝人　　C

3. 助理只是艾倫暫時的工作，他計畫在一家跨國公司找到長期
   的職位。
   (A) 逐漸的　(B) 先前的　(C) 合適的　(D) 暫時的　　D

4. 酸雨導致地面釋出有毒物質，植物和樹木因此漸漸遭受污
   染。
   (A) 不生育的　(B) 繁盛的　(C) 有毒的　(D) 疲乏的　　C

公職精選歷屆 必考字彙題

5. This coffee shop is famous because it sells numerous varieties of coffee beans _____ from around the world.
(A) departed (B) imported (C) prevented (D) suffered

6. The factory workers _____ that their workload was too heavy but the pay was too low. They decided to stage a protest.
(A) complained (B) expected (C) introduced (D) proposed

7. The field is too barren to yield crops, so the farmers decide to put some _____ on it.
(A) cuisines (B) fertilizers (C) viruses (D) poisons

8. Athletes always wear clothes made of _____ materials, so they may stretch their bodies without difficulty.
(A) elastic (B) plastic (C) realistic (D) electric

9. The Spanish Flu _____ from 1918 to 1920 claimed over thirty million lives around the world.
(A) academy (B) vaccination (C) disruption (D) epidemic

10. This handmade car sold for a million dollars because it was _____.
(A) familiar (B) commonplace (C) unique (D) widespread

11. In the _____ of anyone better, we chose him as the leader.
(A) problem (B) question (C) absence (D) objective

12. The congressman's first public speech was _____. The day after his speech, tens of thousands of people gathered in the capital to protest against his racist remarks.
(A) monotonous (B) controversial (C) plain (D) protective

答案

5. 這家咖啡店很有名,因為販賣很多世界各地進口的咖啡豆。
   (A) 啓程 (B) 進口 (C) 預防 (D) 受苦　　　　　B

6. 工廠工人抱怨工作量太重而薪水卻太低,他們決定發起抗議。
   (A) 抱怨 (B) 期待 (C) 引進 (D) 提議　　　　　A

7. 田地太荒蕪長不出穀物,因此農夫們決定施些肥料在上面。
   (A) 食品 (B) 肥料 (C) 病毒 (D) 毒物　　　　　B

8. 運動員總是穿著彈性材料製成的衣服,如此他們可以毫無困難伸展全身。
   (A) 有彈力的 (B) 塑膠的 (C) 現實的 (D) 電子的　　　　　A

9. 一九一八至一九二零年間的西班牙流感奪走全世界超過三千萬人的生命。
   (A) 學術 (B) 接種疫苗 (C) 混亂 (D) 傳染病　　　　　D

10.這部手工打造的汽車相當獨特,以一百萬元售出。
   (A) 熟悉的 (B) 平凡的 (C) 獨特的 (D) 廣泛的　　　　　C

11.由於目前缺乏其他更好的人選,因此我們選擇他當領導人。
   (A) 問題 (B) 疑問 (C) 缺少 (D) 目標　　　　　C

12.那位國會議員的首次公開演講掀起爭論,演講後隔天,數萬人聚集首都抗議他帶有種族偏見的言論。
   (A) 單調的 (B) 爭論的 (C) 平淡的 (D) 保護的　　　　　B

13. The secretary was _____ for work because of the heavy traffic.
(A) late (B) hired (C) special (D) quiet

14. Please turn off the light. We should save _____ ; otherwise, the bill might go up again.
(A) engine (B) electricity (C) elevator (D) exhibition

15. When she _____ in track-and-field events in the 1960 Olympics, Wilma Rudolph won three gold medals.
(A) grinned (B) determined (C) defined (D) competed

16. In India, eighty percent of the entire _____ are Hindus.
(A) solution (B) tradition (C) population (D) organization

17. Taipei 101 is one of the most well-known _____ in the world. You can enjoy a great view of the city from the top floors of the building.
(A) companies (B) skyscrapers (C) organizations (D) advertisements

18. Most students think that there is a need to _____ bus fare, but not all students agree to have the fare increased by 35 percent.
(A) raise (B) rise (C) improve (D) invent

19. A restaurant manager should know how to deal with _____ from customers who are not satisfied with the food or the service.
(A) praises (B) complaints (C) responsibility (D) performance

20. That old man has no family, so he sometimes gets very, very _____ .
(A) friendly (B) natural (C) comfortable (D) lonely

13. 那位秘書因為交通擁擠而上班遲到。

(A) 遲到 (B) 受雇 (C) 特別的 (D) 安靜的   V

14. 請關掉電燈。我們應該省電,否則帳單可能又要增加了。

(A) 引擎 (B) 電力 (C) 電梯 (D) 展覽   B

15. 威瑪魯多夫在一九六零年的奧林匹克田徑比賽贏得三面金牌。

(A) 露齒笑 (B) 決定 (C) 下定義 (D) 競賽   D

16. 印度有百分之八十的人是印度教徒。

(A) 解決 (B) 傳統 (C) 人口 (D) 組織   C

17. 台北101是世界上最著名的摩天大樓之一,你可以從建築物頂樓欣賞城市的絕佳風景。

(A) 公司 (B) 摩天大樓 (C) 組織 (D) 廣告   B

18. 大多數學生認為需要提高公車票價,但並非所有學生都同意票價增加百分之三十五。

(A) 提高 (B) 上升 (C) 改善 (D) 發明   V

19. 餐廳經理應該知道如何處理顧客對食物或服務的抱怨。

(A) 讚美 (B) 抱怨 (C) 責任 (D) 表現   B

金榜解析 deal with=cope with=handle 處理

20. 那位老人沒有家人,所以他有時感到非常非常地孤獨。

(A) 友善的 (B) 自然的 (C) 舒適的 (D) 孤獨的   D

字彙題 14

1. Nick: May I speak with Sharon, please?
   Betty: I'm afraid you _____ the wrong number.
   (A) dialed (B) took (C) made (D) sent

2. I was _____ about Mary so I watched her closely.
   (A) interesting (B) strange (C) curious (D) kind

3. I read about the crime in the _____ .
   (A) newspaper (B) television (C) radio (D) calendar

4. I am very thirsty. May I have some more _____ ?
   (A) beef (B) juice (C) pork (D) sauce

5. Women over forty are advised to perform breast _____ for cancer
   every year.
   (A) measurement (B) operation (C) sensing (D) screening

6 Apart from sheer size, India and China differ from neighboring
   "trading states" in another critical aspect: their ambition to be the
   regional superpower in South Asia and East Asia _____ .
   (A) aggressively (B) individually (C) provincially
   (D) respectively

7. You need to _____ the document before signing it.
   (A) undermine (B) fabricate (C) peruse (D) execute

8. J. K. Rowling, author of the popular Harry Potter series, exhibits
   _____ control over her stories.
   (A) intrusive (B) inaccessible (C) impeccable (D) intrinsic

解答 14

1. 尼克：我可以跟雪倫講話嗎?
   貝蒂：你恐怕打錯了。
   (A) 撥 (B) 拿 (C) 製造 (D) 送　　　　　　　　　A

2. 我對瑪莉很好奇，所以仔細地觀察她。
   (A) 有趣的 (B) 奇怪的 (C) 好奇的 (D) 親切的　　C

3. 我在報紙讀到有關那宗犯罪事件。
   (A) 報紙 (B) 電視 (C) 收音機 (D) 日曆　　　　　A

4. 我口好渴，可以再給我一些果汁嗎?
   (A) 牛肉 (B) 果汁 (C) 豬肉 (D) 醬油　　　　　B

5. 一般建議四十歲以後的婦女每年做乳房癌症掃描。
   (A) 測量 (B) 手術 (C) 意識 (D) 掃描　　　　　D

6. 印度和中國除了規模龐大之外，不同於鄰近貿易國的另一評
   論是：他們各自都有野心要成為南亞和東亞的區域強權。
   (A) 挑釁地 (B) 單獨地 (C) 偏狹地 (D) 分別地　　D

7. 簽字之前你需要熟讀文件。
   (A) 沖蝕 (B) 偽造 (C) 熟讀 (D) 實施　　　　　C

8. **J.K.**羅琳是廣受歡迎的哈利波特故事系列作者，她展現對故
   事的完美掌握。
   (A) 侵入的 (B) 達不到的 (C) 無瑕疵的 (D) 內在的　C

9. In my family with Chinese tradition, only Daddy and the oldest brother were allowed individual _____ . Daughters were all expected to be of one standard.
(A) contributions (B) controversies (C) idiosyncrasies
(D) consistencies

10. A _____ hairline at the forehead is a part of the male aging process.
(A) conceding (B) interceding (C) proceeding (D) receding

11. In America, "wellness" has become a huge industry _____ especially to the prosperous discontent of the baby-boomers.
(A) proposing (B) catering (C) deferring (D) referring

12. The tailor-made diet and exercise program are _____ to her health. Her doctor already indicated that her recovery from the surgery was extraordinary.
(A) abrasive (B) conducive (C) ingenious (D) reflective

13. To prove himself not involved in the crime, Tommy has to provide an _____ .
(A) album (B) autonomy (C) alias (D) alibi

14. Taipei 101 is a breathtakingly _____ work of art, a stunning masterpiece of concrete and steel that soars 508 meters into the sky.
(A) audible (B) olfactory (C) strenuous (D) audacious

15. The _____ warnings on cigarette packs aim to remind the smokers of the danger of smoking.
(A) blunt (B) dubious (C) genetic (D) exotic

答案

9. 我的家庭中國傳統色彩濃厚，只有父親及長兄獲准擁有個人特質。女兒都被要求為同一種標準。
   (A) 貢獻 (B) 爭論 (C) 特質 (D) 一致 .... **C**

10. 前額上方後退的髮線是男性老化過程的一部分。
    (A) 讓步的 (B) 調解的 (C) 前進的 (D) 後退的 .... **D**

11. 在美國，「健康」是要特別因應對嬰兒潮的極度不滿，已經成為一項龐大產業。
    (A) 提議 (B) 迎合 (C) 拖延 (D) 有關係 .... **B**

> 金榜解析 cater to 迎合

12. 特製的飲食及運動計畫有助於她的健康，她的醫師已指出她術後恢復得非常好。
    (A) 惹人討厭的 (B) 有助於… (C) 別出心裁的 (D) 反射的 .... **B**

13. 湯米為了證明自己沒有涉案，必須提供一份不在場證明。
    (A) 相簿 (B) 自治權 (C) 化名 (D) 不在場證明 .... **D**

14. 台北101是一座大膽驚人的藝術作品，是一件升入上空五百零八公尺的鋼筋水泥的極佳傑作。
    (A) 聽得見的 (B) 嗅覺的 (C) 盡力的 (D) 大膽的 .... **D**

15. 香菸盒上直率的警語旨在提醒癮君子吸菸的危險。
    (A) 直率的 (B) 猶豫不決的 (C) 遺傳的 (D) 異國的 .... **A**

> 金榜解析 remind 人 of 事 提醒某人關於某事

16. Unemployment anywhere is a _____ on the country's resources.
   (A) drive (B) drain (C) lift (D) sign

17. The _____ guerrilla groups agreed to stop fighting and settle their differences peacefully.
   (A) distilled (B) extradited (C) privy (D) rival

18. Nowadays some people feel sad and suffer from _____ because of high expectation and low achievement.
   (A) depression (B) impression (C) oppression (D) suppression

19. Two of the hostages held inside the auditorium were released yesterday on _____ grounds.
   (A) homogeneous (B) heterogeneous (C) humanitarian
   (D) hypersensitive

20. The office is on the tenth floor. It will be too tiring if we climb the stairs; we'd better take the _____ .
   (A) elevator (B) tram (C) ascender (D) riser

考前衝刺★★★★★

1. My son is _____ of the dark, so he never walks out of the house after sunset.
   (A) angry (B) afraid (C) proud (D) worried

2. Although the artist was only half-Mexican, all her paintings demonstrated her Mexican _____ . She was obviously proud of her roots.
   (A) foreboding (B) identity (C) orientation (D) significance

答案

16. 無論在任何地方，失業都是國家資源的一種浪費。
    (A) 推動 (B) 浪費 (C) 提升 (D) 記號　　　　B

17. 地下游擊組織同意停止戰鬥並和平解決彼此間的歧異。
    (A) 蒸餾 (B) 引渡 (C) 秘密的 (D) 敵對的　　　C

18. 現今有些人因為高期待、低成就感到悲傷，並受憂鬱之苦。
    (A) 憂鬱 (B) 印象 (C) 壓迫 (D) 抑制　　　　A

19. 基於人道理由，禮堂裡其中兩位遭挾持的人質昨天被釋放了。
    (A) 同質的 (B) 異質的 (C) 人道的 (D) 過敏的　C

20. 辦公室在十樓，如果爬樓梯的話會太累，我們最好搭電梯。
    (A) 電梯 (B) 電車 (C) 上升的人 (D) 起床者　A

考前衝刺★★★★★

答案

1. 我兒子怕黑，所以他從未在日落後外出。
   (A) 生氣的 (B) 害怕的 (C) 驕傲的 (D) 擔心的　　B

2. 雖然那位藝術家只是半個墨西哥人，她所有畫作均展現出自身的墨西哥特質，顯然以她的祖先為榮。
   (A) 預兆 (B) 特性 (C) 定位 (D) 意義　　　　B

公職精選歷屆 **必考字彙題**

3. Laura has a _____ to put things off until the last minute.
   (A) disparity (B) fecundity (C) tendency (D) vivacity

4. A recent study finds that newly retired couples report the highest level of marital conflict. The good news is that after two years that tension tends to _____ .
   (A) aggravate (B) diminish (C) merge (D) rotate

5. If you want to lose weight, you should not eat between _____ .
   (A) terms (B) travels (C) meals (D) limits

6. He is addicted to caffeine. Every morning, he will never truly wake up until he sips a cup of freshly _____ coffee.
   (A) squeezed (B) brewed (C) drained (D) cooked

7. Many vineyard owners are concerned that oversupply may cause the _____ prices of wine to drop on the market.
   (A) quota (B) retail (C) surplus (D) tariff

8. Stella is late again; she probably _____ the bus.
   (A) mistook (B) missed (C) changed (D) forgot

9. There is no _____ that Joanna will pass the French exam. She has studied so hard for it.
   (A) idea (B) worry (C) doubt (D) rush

10. My boyfriend doesn't like it if I speak to other boys when we're out. He gets really _____ .
    (A) ambitious (B) jealous (C) religious (D) obvious

11. These products are not for export; they are for _____ market only.
    (A) foreign (B) domestic (C) realistic (D) positive

答案

3. 蘿菈很容易把事情拖延到最後一分鐘。

(A) 不相稱 (B) 創造力 (C) 傾向 (D) 活潑　　　　C

金榜解析 have a tendency to 有…傾向

4. 最近的一份研究發現剛退休的夫婦會有最高程度的婚姻衝突；好消息是兩年後那種緊張情勢會趨於縮小。

(A) 惡化 (B) 縮小 (C) 吞沒 (D) 旋轉　　　　B

5. 如果你要減重,你不該在餐間吃東西。

(A) 學期 (B) 旅行 (C) 餐 (D) 限制　　　　C

6. 他對咖啡因上癮。每天早上,他要啜飲一杯現煮咖啡才會完全清醒。

(A) 擠壓 (B) 釀造 (C) 流出 (D) 煮　　　　D

金榜解析 be addicted to 對…上癮,接名詞或動名詞片語。

7. 許多葡萄園主人擔心過度供應可能導致葡萄酒市場零售價格下跌。

(A) 配額 (B) 零售 (C) 過剩 (D) 稅制　　　　B

8. 史提拉又遲到了;她可能沒趕上公車。

(A) 誤認 (B) 錯過 (C) 改變 (D) 忘記　　　　B

9. 喬安娜毫無疑問會通過法文考試,她一直很努力準備。

(A) 主意 (B) 擔心 (C) 懷疑 (D) 匆促　　　　C

金榜解析 There is no doubt that…無疑地

10. 我男朋友不喜歡我們外出時我跟其他男生講話,他吃醋吃得可兇了。

(A) 野心勃勃的 (B) 嫉妒的 (C) 宗教的 (D) 明顯的　　　　B

11. 這些產品不是要出口的,它們只銷國內市場。

(A) 外國 (B) 國內的 (C) 現實的 (D) 正面的　　　　B

公職精選歷屆必考字彙題

12. Don't think that your computer is safe. Hundreds of thousands of computers might now be _____ to various kinds of powerful viruses.
(A) vulnerable (B) compatible (C) discernible (D) numerable

13. The speaker _____ a short summary of the main points into the ending of her speech.
(A) incapacitates (B) incarcerates (C) incinerates
(D) incorporates

14. Most actors hate _____ reporters because they ask more questions than are necessary or even proper.
(A) inquisitive (B) outspoken (C) talkative (D) verbose

15. Since high-tech industries are in desperate need of electricity supply, the government's _____ is to build more power plants.
(A) fidelity (B) priority (C) finality (D) peculiarity

16. The world's treasures are under _____ as never before. So, get out and see as many as possible before they disappear.
(A) privilege (B) probation (C) siege (D) temptation

17. Don't be so _____ about others' business. You should learn to mind your own business.
(A) fancy (B) nosy (C) mouthy (D) easy

18. Jane's _____ were high with the hope of seeing the Pope in person.
(A) joys (B) minds (C) senses (D) spirits

19. You would not explore the backstreets of a foreign city without a guidebook, nor should you explore online _____ worlds without some local know-how.
(A) serene (B) spacious (C) virtual (D) voracious

12. 不要認為你的電腦是安全的,目前有數十萬部電腦有潛在危險會受到各種強大病毒的攻擊。

(A) 易受攻擊的 (B) 相容的 (C) 可辨識的 (D) 可數的　　A

13. 演說者將一段重點做摘要,併入她演說的結語中。

(A) 使無能力 (B) 入監 (C) 火化 (D) 合併　　D

金榜解析 incorporate…into 將… 併入

14. 大多數演員討厭好問的記者,因為他們會問不必要或不適當的問題。

(A) 好問的 (B) 坦率的 (C) 多話的 (D) 嘮叨的　　A

15. 高科技產業極需電力供應,因此政府的優先要務是興建更多發電廠。

(A) 忠實 (B) 優先順序 (C) 終結 (D) 怪癖　　B

16. 世界上的珍寶是前所未有的誘惑,因此在它們消失之前要盡可能多出去看一看。

(A) 特權 (B) 查驗 (C) 包圍 (D) 引誘　　D

17. 不要那麼好管閒事,你該學著管好自己的事情。

(A) 精心設計的 (B) 好管閒事的 (C) 多嘴的 (D) 容易的　　B

18. 珍的心情亢奮,因為她有望能親自見到教皇。

(A) 喜樂 (B) 心思 (C) 感官 (D) 心情　　D

19. 不要沒有旅行指南就去探索一個外國城市的小街,也不該在沒有一些當地技術就在網路上探索虛擬世界。

(A) 平靜的 (B) 寬敞的 (C) 虛擬的 (D) 貪婪的　　C

公職精選歷屆 必考字彙題

20. Alex is the youngest child in his family. His parents always treat
    him like a baby and expect him to behave _____ .
    (A) accordingly (B) knowingly (C) simultaneously
    (D) subsequently

考前衝刺★★★★★

1. Being a tour guide is a very important job. In many cases, the tour
    guide is the traveler's first _____ of our country.
    (A) difference (B) impression (C) dictation (D) influence

2. Parents should teach their children to _____ their money at an
    early age. Otherwise, when they grow up, they will not know how
    to manage their money.
    (A) inspire (B) budget (C) instill (D) assert

3. To make the best use of your time, you have to list your goals in
    order of _____ .
    (A) privation (B) privacy (C) priority (D) privilege

4. Many contemporary people have _____ illness caused not by
    physical problem but by mental stress.
    (A) psychoanalytic (B) psychochemical (C) psychosomatic
    (D) psychotherapeutic

5. The _____ floods in the southern provinces of the Netherlands
    have been the worst since the great North Sea floods of 1953.
    (A) contentious (B) contagious (C) collapsing (D) catastrophic

20. 艾雷斯是家中的老么，他父母總是對待他像個嬰兒，又期待
他表現得懂事一點。

答案

(A) 相應地 (B) 老練地 (C) 同時地 (D) 其次　　　　　　B

考前衝刺★★★★★

答案

1. 導遊是一份非常重要的工作。許多狀況中，導遊是旅客對我
們國家的第一印象。

(A) 不同 (B) 印象 (C) 聽寫 (D) 影響　　　　　　B

2. 家長應該在孩子年幼時教他們作收支預算，否則他們長大後
會不知道如何管理自身財務。

(A) 鼓舞 (B) 編預算 (C) 使滲透 (D) 聲明　　　　　　B

3. 爲了能最妥善利用時間，你必須按優先順序列出你的目標。

(A) 窮困 (B) 隱私 (C) 優先次序 (D) 特權　　　　　　C

4. 許多現代人有身心失調的疾病，但並非生理問題，而是心理
壓力造成的。

(A) 精神分析的 (B) 精神化學的 (C) 身心失調的 (D) 精神療法的 C

5. 自一九五三年北海的洪水泛濫之後，荷蘭南部省分災難性的
水災一直是最嚴重的。

(A) 愛爭論的 (B) 傳染性的 (C) 崩潰的 (D) 大災難的　　　　　　D

6. The mountain climbers were _____ by a storm and had to stay in the cabin for three days.
   (A) confirmed (B) stained (C) stranded (D) suppressed

7. The government promised to _____ a new system to control financial loan institutions.
   (A) implement (B) interfere (C) immerse (D) infer

8. Sarah gave me very _____ directions to her house, but somehow I still couldn't find my way there.
   (A) ambiguous (B) explicit (C) illicit (D) pernicious

9. Many husbands have _____ feelings about their wives with successful careers. They may be proud of what their wives do, but they may also feel neglected, threatened, or even resentful.
   (A) ambivalent (B) capricious (C) empathic (D) asymmetric

10. Collecting seems to be such a _____ activity that it is almost hard to find someone who does not collect something.
   (A) unique (B) luxurious (C) rare (D) widespread

11. The publication is only available by _____. In other words, it is not sold in any store.
   (A) subsidence (B) subscription (C) subsidiary (D) substance

12. It took years to _____ the legal complexities of the case.
   (A) untangle (B) detonate (C) refute (D) renovate

13. I can feel that he wants to do something bad to me from his _____ glare.
   (A) maladroit (B) malignant (C) malodorous (D) malnourished

答案

6. 登山客受困於暴風雨必須在小屋待上三天。
   (A) 確認 (B) 玷汙 (C) 處於困境 (D) 鎮壓　　　　　C

7. 政府承諾實施一項管控金融貸款機構的新制度。
   (A) 實施 (B) 干涉 (C) 沉浸 (D) 推論　　　　　　A

8. 莎拉明確指引我到她家的方向，但我還是找不到路。
   (A) 模擬兩可的 (B) 明確的 (C) 違法的 (D) 有害的　B

9. 許多丈夫對事業成功的妻子有矛盾情感。他們可能會替妻子
   事業成功而驕傲，但也可能感覺遭忽略、受威脅，甚至感到
   怨恨。
   (A) 有矛盾情感的 (B) 任性的 (C) 移情作用的 (D) 不對稱的　A

10. 收藏似乎是一項廣泛的活動，幾乎很難找到不收集東西的
    人。
    (A) 獨特的 (B) 奢侈的 (C) 罕見的 (D) 廣泛的　　D

11. 那本出版物只能訂閱。換句話說，它不在任何商店販售。
    (A) 沉澱 (B) 訂購 (C) 補助的 (D) 物質　　　　　B

12. 這案件花了好幾年才將其法律複雜性解開。
    (A) 解開 (B) 觸發 (C) 駁斥 (D) 革新　　　　　　A

13. 從他惡意的目光可以感受到他要對我做出不利的事。
    (A) 拙劣的 (B) 有惡意的 (C) 有惡臭的 (D) 營養不良的　B

14. In present-day Hawaii, there are at least twelve different _____ groups. None of these is large enough to form a majority of the population.
(A) ethical (B) ethnic (C) heterosexual (D) homosexual

15. Fortunately, the man _____ to escape before the old building collapsed.
(A) commanded (B) hesitated (C) managed (D) pretended

16. Miss Young is very _____ with her students so they are all afraid of her.
(A) kind (B) strict (C) lazy (D) confused

17. In some places, people still need the assistance of an _____ to make a long-distance call.
(A) engineer (B) amateur (C) athlete (D) operator

18. It's easy to get around the city because it has a very good transportation _____ .
(A) level (B) system (C) society (D) instrument

19. John's ideas are simply ridiculous! I don't see how any _____ person could agree with him.
(A) sensitive (B) stable (C) superior (D) sensible

20. Just _____ something when you forget your speech.
(A) impress (B) imprison (C) improve (D) improvise

答案

14. 現今夏威夷至少有十二個不同族群,但沒有一個大到足以形成多數人口。

    (A) 倫理的 (B) 種族的 (C) 異性的 (D) 同性的　　　　**B**

15. 幸好那名男子在舊建築物倒塌前設法躲開了。

    (A) 命令 (B) 猶豫 (C) 設法做到 (D) 假裝　　　　**C**

金榜解析 **manage to 設法做到**

16. 楊老師對學生非常嚴格,所以學生都很怕她。

    (A) 種類 (B) 嚴格的 (C) 懶惰的 (D) 困惑的　　　　**B**

金榜解析 **be strict with 對…嚴格**

17. 人們在某些地方仍需總機的協助才能打長途電話。

    (A) 工程師 (B) 業餘選手 (C) 運動員 (D) 總機人員　　　　**D**

18. 暢遊這座城市十分容易,因為大眾運輸系統很發達。

    (A) 水準 (B) 系統 (C) 社會 (D) 儀器　　　　**B**

19. 約翰的想法簡直荒謬!我想任何一個明智的人都不會認同。

    (A) 敏感的 (B) 穩定的 (C) 優秀的 (D) 明智的　　　　**D**

20. 當你忘記要說的話時,就隨手記下一些東西。

    (A) 印記 (B) 監禁 (C) 促進 (D) 即席寫作　　　　**D**

字彙題 17

1. The members of the older _____ do not understand why young people like to go to such noisy places as KTVs.
   (A) destruction (B) identification (C) glorification (D) generation

2. Her daughter's _____ to her makes her very sad. She wishes her daughter would show more concern for her.
   (A) institution (B) preference (C) indifference (D) addition

3. Neither Chinese nor American government is under any illusion that the trade imbalance between the two countries will soon be _____ .
   (A) dignified (B) rectified (C) specified (D) verified

4. Mary broke up with George mainly because she could not stand his _____ language and rude behavior to her parents.
   (A) remorse (B) vainglorious (C) physical (D) vulgar

5. It is a _____ of our time in the West that never have so many people been so relatively well off and never has society been more troubled.
   (A) maxim (B) credibility (C) ambiguity (D) paradox

6. Bird _____ has killed more than 60 people in Southeast Asia since it was first discovered in 2003.
   (A) flight (B) flu (C) feather (D) flow

7. Penguins have _____ but they cannot fly.
   (A) legs (B) wings (C) eyes (D) nests

8. The photographer _____ the photos in his own laboratory.
   (A) develops (B) hires (C) sends (D) realizes

解答 17

答案

1. 老一輩的人不懂為何年輕人愛去**KTV**這類吵雜的地方。
   (A) 破壞 (B) 認出 (C) 稱讚 (D) 世代　　　　　　　　　D

2. 她女兒的漠不關心令她非常傷心，她希望女兒對她表現出更
   多的關心。
   (A) 習慣 (B) 偏好 (C) 漠不關心 (D) 增加　　　　　　　C

3. 中國或美國都不該存有幻想，以為兩國的貿易逆差很快就能
   矯正過來。
   (A) 使高貴 (B) 矯正 (C) 詳細說明 (D) 證實　　　　　　B

4. 瑪莉和喬治分手了，因為她無法忍受他對她父母粗野的言語
   及粗魯的行為。
   (A) 自責 (B) 自負的 (C) 生理的 (D) 粗野的　　　　　　D

5. 我們這年代的西方國家正處於矛盾狀態，從來沒有這麼多富
   可敵國的人，也沒有一個比當今更為混亂的社會。
   (A) 準則 (B) 可信度 (C) 歧異 (D) 矛盾　　　　　　　　D

6. 禽流感自二千零三年首次發現後，已在東南亞奪走超過六十
   多條人命。
   (A) 飛行 (B) 流行性感冒 (C) 羽毛 (D) 流動　　　　　　B

7. 企鵝有翅膀，但是它們不會飛。
   (A) 腿 (B) 翅膀 (C) 眼睛 (D) 鳥巢　　　　　　　　　　B

8. 攝影師在自己的實驗室沖洗相片。
   (A) 沖洗 (B) 雇用 (C) 寄送 (D) 了解　　　　　　　　　A

公職精選歷屆 **必考**字彙題

9. The National Palace Museum opens daily from 9 a.m. to 5 p.m.. However, for Saturdays, the hours are _____ to 8:30 p.m..
   (A) closed (B) moved (C) lasted (D) extended

10. I love getting up at _____. Watching the sunrise is the best way to start the day.
    (A) dawn (B) noon (C) midnight (D) night

11. The museum has a marvelous _____ of art works from all over the world.
    (A) distance (B) mixture (C) connection (D) degree

12. The driver has made a _____ that you throw all your garbage in the bin at the front on your way out.
    (A) license (B) fence (C) fossil (D) request

13. In order to _____ the architecture of the building, you really need to get off the bus and get closer to it.
    (A) absorb (B) exhaust (C) beware (D) appreciate

14. Giant pandas are among the _____ animals in the world. There are only some 1,860 in the world, and two are residing in Taipei Zoo now.
    (A) busiest (B) rarest (C) smartest (D) barest

15. Taking photographs inside the museum is _____. However, you can take pictures of the grounds and the outside of the buildings.
    (A) diagnosed (B) prohibited (C) recruited (D) exploded

16. We don't recommend exchanging your money at the hotel because you won't get a _____ rate.
    (A) humble (B) partial (C) dull (D) fair

9. 國立故宮博物院平日是早上九點開放到下午五點，但週六開放時間延長到晚上八點半。
   (A) 關閉 (B) 移動 (C) 持續 (D) 延長　　　　　　　　　　D

10. 我喜愛在黎明起床，觀看日出是展開一天的最好方法。
    (A) 黎明 (B) 正中午 (C) 半夜 (D) 夜晚　　　　　　　　A

11. 這家博物館有來自世界各地藝術作品的美妙融合。
    (A) 距離 (B) 混合 (C) 連結 (D) 程度　　　　　　　　　B

12. 司機要求你將所有垃圾丟在出口前面的垃圾桶裡。
    (A) 執照 (B) 圍籬 (C) 化石 (D) 要求　　　　　　　　　D

金榜解析 you throw all your garbage，省略了 you (should) throw
表示要求request時應搭配含should的假設語氣。

13. 為了欣賞這座建築物的建築風格，你需要下車多靠近點看。
    (A) 吸收 (B) 排氣 (C) 注意 (D) 欣賞　　　　　　　　　D

14. 貓熊是世界上最稀有的動物之一。現在世界上只有一千八百六十隻左右，其中兩隻在木柵動物園。
    (A) 最忙碌 (B) 最稀有 (C) 最聰明 (D) 最赤裸的　　　　B

15. 博物館裡禁止照相，不過你可以拍地面及建築物外觀。
    (A) 診斷 (B) 禁止 (C) 招募 (D) 爆炸　　　　　　　　　B

16. 我們不建議你在飯店換錢，因為你得不到合理的匯率。
    (A) 謙卑的 (B) 部分的 (C) 愚蠢的 (D) 合理的　　　　　D

17. Baseball is the number one team sport here in Taiwan. The most accomplished player, New York Yankees' Wang Chien-ming, is _____ referred to as a national treasure.
(A) barely (B) frequently (C) hardly (D) thinly

18. The first sign of autumn is that the temperature has a _____ change between morning and night, coming down from 30 degrees to around 20 degrees Celsius.
(A) small (B) trivial (C) significant (D) mild

19. Caused by the _____ of our "body clock", jet lag can be a big problem for most travelers in the first few days after they have arrived at their destination.
(A) aspiration (B) inspiration (C) disruption (D) motivation

20. More and more Taiwanese have come to view cycling not only as a form of recreation but as a way of being environmentally _____.
(A) friendly (B) guilty (C) ignorant (D) bizarre

考前衝刺★★★★★

1. Hotels are _____ internationally from one to five stars, depending on the services they offer and the prices of rooms.
(A) decorated (B) elevated (C) ranked (D) advised

2. The travel agent says that we have to pay a deposit of $2,000 in advance in order to _____ the reservation for our hotel room.
(A) cancel (B) protect (C) remove (D) secure

答案

17. 棒球在台灣是排行第一的團隊運動。紐約洋基隊的王建民是
最有成就的選手，經常被視為國寶。
(A) 赤裸裸地 (B) 經常地 (C) 幾乎不 (D) 稀少地　　　**B**

18. 早晚溫度變化明顯是秋天來臨的第一個跡象，氣溫會從攝氏
三十度下降到大約二十度。
(A) 小的 (B) 微不足道的 (C) 明顯的 (D) 適中的　　　**C**

19. 大部分的旅客剛抵達目的地的那幾天會有時差的問題，這是
由於生理時鐘混亂所導致的。
(A) 渴望 (B) 靈感 (C) 混亂 (D) 動機　　　**C**

20. 越來越多台灣人不僅將單車旅行視為一種休閒型態，也是一
種對環境有益的方式。
(A) 友善的 (B) 有罪的 (C) 無知的 (D) 古怪的　　　**A**

考前衝刺★★★★

答案

1. 依照所提供的服務及房價，國際上將飯店分為一到五個星
級。
(A) 裝飾 (B) 提升 (C) 劃分等級 (D) 勸告　　　**C**

2. 旅行社說我們須事先支付訂金二千元確保我們飯店的訂房。
(A) 取消 (B) 保護 (C) 移除 (D) 確保　　　**D**

公職精選歷屆 **必考字彙題**

3. Display this parking _____ on your window to show that you are a hotel guest.
   (A) grant (B) privilege (C) garage (D) pass

4. When I take a flight, I always ask for _____ seat, so it is easier for me to get up and walk around.
   (A) a window (B) a cabinet (C) a middle (D) an aisle

5. With 49 shops around the island, Eslite Bookstore was _____ by Time magazine in 2004 as a must-see for visitors to Taiwan.
   (A) charged (B) selected (C) discredited (D) accused

6. Because of its inexpensive yet high-quality medical services, medical tourism is _____ in Taiwan.
   (A) declining (B) blowing (C) booming (D) collapsing

7. Table manners differ from culture to culture. In Italy, it is considered _____ for a woman to pour her neighbor a glass of wine.
   (A) inappropriate (B) inconsistent (C) incomplete (D) infinite

8. "Flight AB123 to Tokyo has been delayed. Please check the monitor for _____ information about your departure time."
   (A) further (B) optional (C) fluent (D) inside

9. Ku-Kuan, east of Taichung City, with its steep cliffs, has become a _____ for rock climbers here in Taiwan.
   (A) victory (B) paradise (C) competition (D) factory

10. The $3,600 shopping voucher program was _____ to spur domestic consumption, and for most people, these vouchers are really "gifts from heaven".
    (A) inspected (B) complied (C) contained (D) designed

3. 把停車通行證放在車窗上以顯示你是飯店房客。

   (A) 許可　(B) 特權　(C) 停車場　(D) 通行證　　　　　D

4. 搭飛機時，我總是要求走道座位，這樣較能輕易起身到處走動。

   (A) 窗戶　(B) 機艙　(C) 中央　(D) 走道　　　　　D

5. 誠品書局在全台共有四十九家店，二千零四年時代雜誌評選為來台遊客必訪之處。

   (A) 控訴　(B) 選擇　(C) 給予恥辱　(D) 告發　　　　　B

   金榜解析 be elected as 被選為…

6. 因為高貴不貴的醫藥服務，醫療觀光業在台灣蓬勃發展。

   (A) 下降　(B) 吹動　(C) 繁榮　(D) 衰退　　　　　C

   金榜解析 because of=owing to 因為

7. 餐桌禮儀因文化而不同。在義大利，婦女不宜替鄰坐的人倒酒。

   (A) 不適宜　(B) 不一致　(C) 不完全　(D) 無數的　　　　　A

8. 往東京的 **AB123** 班機已經誤點，要知道起飛時間的進一步訊息，請檢視螢幕。

   (A) 進一步的　(B) 選擇的　(C) 流利的　(D) 內部的　　　　　A

   金榜解析 further information 進一步消息
   　　　　　further study 進修
   　　　　　further notice 進一步通知

9. 谷關位於台中市的東方，因陡峭懸崖而成為台灣攀岩者的天堂。

   (A) 勝利　(B) 天堂　(C) 競爭　(D) 工廠　　　　　B

10. 台幣三千六百元的消費券計畫是設計來刺激國內消費，對大部份人來說，這些消費券真是「天上掉下來的禮物」。

    (A) 檢查　(B) 同意　(C) 包含　(D) 設計　　　　　D

11. When Americans shake hands, they do so firmly, not loosely. In the American culture, a weak handshake is a sign of weak _____.
(A) personnel (B) currency (C) character (D) parade

12. When Latin Americans and Middle Easterners _____ each other, they tend to stand closer together when talking than Americans do.
(A) ignore (B) greet (C) criticize (D) plow

13. In most western countries, it's _____ for you to bring a bottle of wine or a box of candy as a gift when you are invited for dinner at someone's home.
(A) temporary (B) invalid (C) customary (D) stubborn

14. It takes both experience and careful _____ in order to become aware of what people in different cultures see as a "normal" or "natural" behavior.
(A) obstruction (B) paradox (C) prevention (D) observation

15. During the holidays, most major hotels will be fully booked. An _____ is to try and find a guest house near your desired destination.
(A) exchange (B) alternative (C) equivalent (D) applause

16. A total of 3,965 athletes from 81 countries will compete in the 21st Summer Deaflympics to be _____ by Taipei City from September 5 to September 15 this year.
(A) fastened (B) hosted (C) offered (D) anchored

17. Barcelona is beautiful but it's always _____ with tourists in the summer.
(A) packed (B) steamed (C) frequented (D) patronized

11. 美國人握手時，都會緊握不鬆手，輕輕握手在美國文化中是軟弱性格的表現。

(A) 人事 (B) 流通 (C) 性格 (D) 遊行　　　　　　　C

12. 拉丁美洲和中東人彼此問候時，他們談話時的距離往往比美國人更近。

(A) 忽視 (B) 迎接 (C) 批評 (D) 費力地通過　　　B

13. 在大部分西方國家，當你受邀到某人家中晚餐時，帶一瓶酒或一盒糖果當作禮物是合乎禮俗的。

(A) 暫時的 (B) 無效的 (C) 合乎禮俗的 (D) 固執的　　C

14. 要了解不同文化的人所認為的「正常」或「自然」行為，需要靠經驗和仔細的觀察。

(A) 阻礙 (B) 正統 (C) 預防 (D) 觀察　　　　　　D

15. 大部分的飯店在假日期間會被預訂一空，另一種替代方案是想法子在你想去的目的地附近找民宿。

(A) 交換 (B) 選擇 (C) 同等物 (D) 喝采　　　　　B

16. 來自八十一個國家，總數三千九百六十五位選手將於今年九月五日至九月十日在台北市主辦的第二十一屆夏季聽障奧運會中一較高下。

(A) 繫上 (B) 主辦 (C) 提供 (D) 固定　　　　　　B

17. 巴塞隆納景色優美，但夏季總是擠滿了觀光客。

(A) 擁擠 (B) 蒸 (C) 時常出入 (D) 贊助　　　　　A

金榜解析 **be packed with** 擠滿了

18. We were asked by our tour guide on the shuttle bus to _____ seated until we reached our destination.
    (A) endure (B) maintain (C) remain (D) adhere

19. Travelers should familiarize themselves with their destinations, both to get the most enjoyment out of the visit and to _____ known dangers.
    (A) neglect (B) interrupt (C) avoid (D) anticipate

20. Some tourists like to make plans and reservations for local tours after they have arrived. They prefer not to have every day of their vacation planned _____.
    (A) behind (B) afterward (C) late (D) ahead

考前衝刺★★★★★

1. Taiwan has more than 400 museums. The most famous of these is the National Palace Museum, which holds the world's largest _____ of Chinese art treasures.
   (A) supply (B) catalogue (C) collection (D) addition

2. Starting in 2005, the Taipei City Government began holding its annual international Beef Noodle Soup Festival to _____ the local favorite to visitors.
   (A) encourage (B) promote (C) develop (D) abandon

3. A website set up by the Taipei Zoo for the two pandas crashed at times as too many Taiwanese tried to catch a _____ of the two cute animals.
   (A) glimpse (B) hold (C) glummer (D) photo

18. 短程巴士上導遊要求我們一直坐著，直到到達目的地為止。
   (A) 容忍 (B) 維修 (C) 保持 (D) 堅持　　　　　　　C

19. 旅客應該熟悉他們的目的地，既能從參訪中得到最大歡樂，
   也能避開預知的危險。
   (A) 忽視 (B) 打斷 (C) 避免 (D) 期待　　　　　　　C

20. 有些觀光客喜歡在抵達後才計畫預訂當地的旅遊，他們較不
   喜歡預先計劃每日的假期。
   (A) 之後 (B) 後來 (C) 遲到 (D) 事先　　　　　　　D

考前衝刺★★★★★

1. 台灣有超過四百座博物館。其中最有名的是故宮博物院，擁
   有世界上最多的中國藝術寶物收藏。
   (A) 供應 (B) 目錄 (C) 收藏 (D) 附加　　　　　　　C

2. 台北市政府於二千零五年開始舉辦年度國際牛肉麵節，向旅
   客推銷當地最夯的食物。
   (A) 鼓勵 (B) 推銷 (C) 發展 (D) 放棄　　　　　　　B

3. 木柵動物園為兩隻大貓熊架設的網站有時候會掛掉，因為太
   多的台灣民眾想要一窺這兩隻可愛的動物。
   (A) 一瞥 (B) 支撐 (C) 憂鬱者 (D) 相片　　　　　　A

金榜解析 catch a glimpse of 一瞥…
take a photo of 照相…

公職精選歷屆
必考字彙題

4. The ＿＿＿ of the New Seven Wonders of the World campaign were announced on July 7th, 2007, and the Great Wall of China is one of the winners.
(A) sources (B) results (C) revolts (D) shelters

5. "One Million Star" is a popular televised singing competition in Taiwan. Every week, the contestants are graded, and the one that performs the worst will be ＿＿＿.
(A) accepted (B) eliminated (C) conserved (D) congratulated

6. The Louvre's Tactile Gallery, specifically designed for the blind and visually ＿＿＿, is the only museum in France where visitors can touch the sculptures.
(A) discounted (B) conducted (C) instructed (D) impaired

7. The World Games of 2009 will take place in Kaohsiung, Taiwan, from July 16th to July 26th. The games will ＿＿＿ sports that are not contested in the Olympic Games.
(A) feature (B) exclaim (C) bloom (D) appeal

8. People with a low ＿＿＿ for spicy food should not try the "Hot and Spicy Chicken Soup" served by this restaurant; it brings tears to my eyes.
(A) prejudice (B) insistence (C) tolerance (D) indulgence

9. Formed in 1991 and having toured internationally in Europe and Asia, the Formosa Aboriginal Dance Troupe is a group that ＿＿＿ Taiwanese folk music.
(A) performs (B) results (C) achieves (D) occurs

10. The two friends wanted to spend their vacation quietly, so they chose a ＿＿＿ village far from busy tourist places.
(A) noisy (B) bustling (C) remote (D) violent

4. 新世界七大奇景活動的結果於二千零七年七月七日宣布，中
國的萬里長城是優勝之一。
(A) 來源 (B) 結果 (C) 叛亂 (D) 庇護所　　　　　　　　　B

5. 「超級星光大道」是台灣受歡迎的歌唱競賽節目。每星期都
會有參賽者晉級，而淘汰表現最糟的那一位。
(A) 接受 (B) 淘汰 (C) 保存 (D) 恭喜　　　　　　　　　B

6. 羅浮宮的觸覺展廳是特別爲視障及視覺受損者設計，也是法
國唯一能讓參觀者觸摸雕塑品的博物館。
(A) 減價 (B) 管理 (C) 指導 (D) 損傷　　　　　　　　　D

7. 二千零九世界運動會將於七月十六日至二十六日在台灣高雄
舉行，比賽將以奧運競賽所沒有的運動項目爲其特色。
(A) 以…爲特色 (B) 大聲責罵 (C) 開花 (D) 吸引　　　　A

8. 無法忍受辛辣食物的人別嘗試這家餐廳的「麻辣雞湯」，它
會讓我飆淚。
(A) 偏見 (B) 堅持 (C) 容忍 (D) 放任　　　　　　　　　C

9. 成立於一九九一年的原舞者是一支表演台灣民俗音樂的團
體，已在歐洲及亞洲國際巡迴演出。
(A) 表現 (B) 結果 (C) 達成 (D) 發生　　　　　　　　　A

10.那兩位友人想安靜地渡假，因此選擇一個遠離熱鬧觀光景點
的偏遠村莊。
(A) 吵鬧的 (B) 忙亂的 (C) 遙遠的 (D) 暴力的　　　　　C

公職精選歷屆
必考字彙題

11. A store named "Come In and Look Around" sold a _____ of things. There were shoes, toys, food, books, and even cameras.
(A) dose (B) shortage (C) fume (D) variety

12. With the international car exhibition on this week, it may be _____ to find parking spaces.
(A) legal (B) smooth (C) tough (D) practical

13. This monument _____ the men and women who died during the war.
(A) presides (B) honors (C) monitors (D) memorizes

14. The hostess _____ the guests to the living room where drinks were served.
(A) clutched (B) resided (C) ushered (D) derived

15. The doctor thought she could never walk. But now she can not only walk but run as well. It is really a _____.
(A) priority (B) miracle (C) balance (D) gesture

16. The strange and frightening house is said to be _____. No one has lived in it for fifty years or more.
(A) sought (B) pounded (C) haunted (D) relieved

17. I haven't been to Prague yet. But I am _____ to go there one day.
(A) planning (B) forming (C) predicting (D) framing

18. You are _____ to have a beverage on the bus, but please do not eat any food.
(A) attained (B) denied (C) permitted (D) expired

答案

11. 一間名爲「進來看看」的商店販賣各式各樣的東西，有鞋
子、玩具、食品、書籍，甚至相機。
(A) 一劑 (B) 缺乏 (C) 蒸氣 (D) 各式各樣　　　　　D

金榜解析 a variety of=various 各式各樣的

12. 因爲這週有國際車展，可能很難找到停車位。
(A) 合法的 (B) 順利的 (C) 困難的 (D) 實際的　　　　C

13. 這座紀念碑是用來對戰爭期間喪命的男士與女士表示敬意。
(A) 管理 (B) 給予榮譽 (C) 監控 (D) 記憶　　　　　B

14. 女主人引領客人到客廳，那裡有供應飲料。
(A) 抓牢 (B) 居住 (C) 引領 (D) 衍生　　　　　　C

15. 以前醫生認爲她永遠不能走路，但是現在她不僅能走又能
跑，眞是奇蹟。
(A) 優先 (B) 奇蹟 (C) 平衡 (D) 姿勢　　　　　　B

16. 那棟詭異又恐怖的房子據說鬧鬼，已經五十多年沒人住在裡
面了。
(A) 尋找 (B) 重擊 (C) 鬧鬼的 (D) 緩和　　　　　C

金榜解析 be said to 據說…

17. 我還沒去過布拉格，但是我正計畫有一天要去那裏。
(A) 計畫 (B) 形成 (C) 預測 (D) 建造　　　　　　A

18. 你可以在公車上喝飲料，但請勿吃任何食物。
(A) 獲得 (B) 否認 (C) 允許 (D) 到期　　　　　　C

金榜解析 be permitted to 允許做…

19. John: If you have any questions while we're going along, please don't _____ to ask.
    Bob: I have a question actually. Where's the best place to have dinner around here?
    (A) remain (B) hesitate (C) delay (D) remind

20. As a tour guide, you will face new _____ every day. One of the hardest parts of your job may be answering questions.
    (A) dooms (B) challenges (C) margins (D) floods

考前衝刺 ★ ★ ★ ★ ★

1. You will have to pay extra _____ for overweight baggage.
   (A) tags (B) badges (C) fees (D) credits

2. If you want to become a successful tour manager, you have to work _____ and learn from the seniors.
   (A) hard (B) hardly (C) harshly (D) easily

3. You will get a boarding _____ after completing the check-in.
   (A) pass (B) post (C) plan (D) past

4. May I have two hundred U.S. dollars in small _____?
   (A) accounts (B) balance (C) numbers (D) denominations

5. The flight to Chicago has been _____ due to heavy snow.
   (A) concealed (B) cancelled (C) compared (D) consoled

6. You will need to take a _____ flight from Taoyuan to Kaohsiung.
   (A) contacting (B) connecting (C) competing (D) computing

答案

19. 約翰：如果在我們同行途中有任何問題，請不要猶豫發問。

　　包伯：我確實有一個問題。這附近哪裡有吃晚餐的最佳選擇？

　　(A) 保留 (B) 猶豫 (C) 延遲 (D) 提醒　　　　　　　　**B**

金榜解析 remind 人 to 提醒某人…

20. 做為一名導遊，你每天會面對新的挑戰，工作最難的部分之一就是回答問題。

　　(A) 惡運 (B) 挑戰 (C) 邊緣 (D) 洪水　　　　　　　　**B**

考前衝刺★★★★★

答案

1. 你要為超重的行李支付額外費用。

　　(A) 標籤 (B) 徽章 (C) 費用 (D) 學分　　　　　　　　**C**

2. 如果要成為一位成功的旅遊經理，你必須努力工作並且向資深人員學習。

　　(A) 努力地 (B) 幾乎不 (C) 刺耳地 (D) 輕易地　　　　**A**

3. 完成報到之後，你會拿到一張登機證。

　　(A) 通行證 (B) 職位 (C) 計畫 (D) 過去　　　　　　　**A**

4. 我可以有小額的兩百美元嗎？

　　(A) 帳單 (B) 結餘 (C) 數字 (D) 票面金額　　　　　　**D**

5. 前往芝加哥的班機因大雪而取消。

　　(A) 隱藏 (B) 取消 (C) 比較 (D) 慰問　　　　　　　　**B**

金榜解析 due to =because of 因為

6. 你需要搭桃園到高雄的轉接班機。

　　(A) 聯絡 (B) 連接 (C) 競爭 (D) 計算　　　　　　　　**B**

公職精選歷屆 **必考字彙題**

7. Many tourists are fascinated by the natural _____ of Taroko Gorge.
(A) sparkles (B) spectacles (C) spectators (D) sprinklers

8. City _____ are always available at the local tourist information center.
(A) floors (B) streets (C) maps (D) tickets

9. The American government has decided to provide financial assistance to _____ the automobile industry. Car makers are relieved at the news.
(A) accommodate (B) bail out (C) cash in on (D) detect

10. Tourists are advised to _____ traveling to areas with landslides.
(A) avoid (B) assume (C) assist (D) accompany

11. All transportation vehicles should be well-____ and kept in good running condition.
(A) retrained (B) maintained (C) entertained (D) suspended

12. _____ birds are suspected to be major carriers of avian flu.
(A) Immigrating (B) Migratory (C) Seasoning (D) Motivating

13. My boss is very _____; he keeps asking us to complete assigned tasks within the limited time span.
(A) luxurious (B) demanding (C) obvious (D) relaxing

14. I missed the early morning train because I _____.
(A) overbooked (B) overcooked (C) overtook (D) overslept

15. In time of economic _____, many small companies will downsize their operation.
(A) appreciation (B) progression (C) recession (D) reduction

答案

7. 許多觀光客對太魯閣的天然景象感到著迷。
   (A) 閃光 (B) 景象 (C) 觀眾 (D) 灑水裝置　　　　　**B**

8. 城市地圖能在當地遊客資訊中心取得。
   (A) 樓層 (B) 街道 (C) 地圖 (D) 門票　　　　　**C**

9. 美國政府已經決定提供金融協助借貸給汽車業，這消息讓汽
   車製造商感到安心。
   (A) 借貸 (B) 保釋 (C) 利用 (D) 發覺　　　　　**A**

10. 告知觀光客避免到有土石流的地區旅遊。
    (A) 避免 (B) 臆測 (C) 協助 (D) 陪伴　　　　　**A**

11. 所有交通運輸工具都應妥善維修並保持良好運作狀況。
    (A) 再訓練 (B) 維修 (C) 娛樂 (D) 中止　　　　　**B**

12. 候鳥疑似是禽流感的主要病媒。
    (A) 遷移 (B) 移棲的 (C) 曬乾 (D) 誘導　　　　　**B**

13. 我老闆的要求很高，他一直要我們在有限的時間內完成指定
    的工作。
    (A) 奢侈的 (B) 要求的 (C) 明顯的 (D) 鬆弛的　　　　　**B**

14. 我因為睡過頭而錯過今天早晨的火車。
    (A) 超量預訂 (B) 煮過熟 (C) 眺望 (D) 睡過頭　　　　　**D**

15. 在經濟衰退時期，許多小公司將精簡營運規模。
    (A) 欣賞 (B) 進展 (C) 衰退 (D) 降低　　　　　**C**

公職精選歷屆
必考字彙題

16. You will be _____ for littering in public places.
    (A) fined (B) found (C) founded (D) funded

17. The police officer needs to _____ the traffic during the rush hours.
    (A) assign (B) break (C) compete (D) direct

18. The hotel services are far from satisfactory. I need to _____ a complaint with the manager.
    (A) pay (B) claim (C) file (D) add

19. The company is _____ the new products now, so you can buy one and get the second one free.
    (A) forwarding (B) progressing (C) promoting (D) pretending

20. Beware of strangers at the airport and do not leave your luggage _____.
    (A) unanswered (B) uninterested (C) unimportant
    (D) unattended

考前衝刺★★★★★

1. If you have the receipts for the goods you have purchased, you can claim a tax _____ at the airport upon departure.
   (A) relief (B) rebate (C) involve (D) reply

2. We are sorry. All lines are currently busy. Please _____ on for the next available agent.
   (A) keep (B) hold (C) call (D) take

3. All passengers shall go through _____ check before boarding.
   (A) security (B) activity (C) insurance (D) deficiency

答案

16. 你會因為在公共場所丟垃圾受罰。

(A) 罰款 (B) 發現 (C) 創立 (D) 提供基金 　　　　　A

17. 警察需要在尖峰時間指揮交通。

(A) 指定 (B) 破壞 (C) 競爭 (D) 指揮 　　　　　D

18. 這家飯店的服務令人很不滿意，我要向經理提出抱怨。

(A) 支付 (B) 聲稱 (C) 提出 (D) 增加 　　　　　C

金榜解析 **file a complain** 提出抱怨

19. 公司正在促銷新產品，你可以買一送一。

(A) 推進 (B) 前進 (C) 推廣 (D) 假裝 　　　　　C

20. 在機場要小心陌生人，不要把你的行李丟著沒人看管。

(A) 無回答的 (B) 漠不關心的 (C) 不重要的 (D) 沒人管的 　　　D

考前衝刺★★★★★

答案

1. 如果你有購物收據，離境時可以在機場要求退稅。

(A) 解除 (B) 折扣 (C) 涉及 (D) 回應 　　　　　A

2. 我們很抱歉，所有線路目前忙線中，請等候下一位可接聽人員。

(A) 保持 (B) 不掛斷 (C) 打電話 (D) 拿取 　　　　　B

金榜解析 **hold on** 不掛斷電話

3. 所有的旅客登機前要通過安全檢查。

(A) 安全 (B) 活動 (C) 保證 (D) 短缺 　　　　　A

公職精選歷屆 **必考字彙題**

4. The time _____ is thirteen hours between Taipei and New York.
(A) decision (B) division (C) diligence (D) difference

5. This artist's _____ are on exhibition at the museum.
(A) workouts (B) presences (C) masterminds (D) masterpieces

6. You will pay a _____ of fifty dollars for your ferry ride.
(A) fan (B) fate (C) fair (D) fare

7. The museum charges adults a small _____ , but children can go in for free.
(A) fee (B) tuition (C) loan (D) ticket

8. The first Taipei Lantern Festival was held in 1990. Due to the event's huge _____, the festival has been expanded every year.
(A) personality (B) popularity (C) exports (D) expenses

9. It is a custom for some Taiwanese to eat a bowl of long noodles on New Year's Eve. They feel that doing so will _____ their chances of living long lives.
(A) save (B) waste (C) delete (D) increase

10. When we get to the airport, we first go to the check-in desk where the airline representatives _____ our luggage.
(A) pack (B) move (C) weigh (D) claim

11. After having been a victim of _____ violence for years, she finally decided to sue her husband for beating her up constantly.
(A) credulous (B) domestic (C) majestic (D) meticulous

12. The school has been granted one million dollars to renovate the library. I am sure the _____ money will give the school library a better appearance.
(A) forthcoming (B) high-living (C) outgoing (D) upbringing

4. 台北和紐約的時差是十三小時。

(A) 決定 (B) 部門 (C) 勤勉 (D) 差異　　　　　　　D

金榜解析 **time difference** 時差

5. 這位藝術家的傑出作品在博物館展出。

(A) 練習 (B) 出席 (C) 主謀 (D) 傑作　　　　　　　D

6. 你要支付五十元交通費搭渡輪。

(A) 電扇 (B) 命運 (C) 市集 (D) 交通費用　　　　　D

7. 博物館向成人收取少許的費用，但兒童可以免費入場。

(A) 費用 (B) 學費 (C) 借款 (D) 門票　　　　　　　A

8. 第一屆台北燈會於一九九零年舉辦，由於活動的超高人氣，
每年都在擴辦。

(A) 人格 (B) 聲望 (C) 出口 (D) 經費　　　　　　　B

9. 除夕吃一碗長壽麵是許多台灣人的習俗，他們覺得這樣會增
加長壽的機會。

(A) 節省 (B) 浪費 (C) 刪除 (D) 增加　　　　　　　D

10. 抵達機場時，我們先去報到櫃台，地勤人員會在那裡過磅我
們的行李。

(A) 包裹 (B) 移動 (C) 秤重 (D) 索償　　　　　　　C

11. 她是多年的家暴受害者，最後終於決定控告她丈夫時常打
她。

(A) 輕易相信的 (B) 家庭的 (C) 高貴的 (D) 拘泥小節的　B

12. 學校授予一百萬元翻新圖書館，我確信這筆即將到來的資金
會帶給學校圖書館一個更好的視野。

(A) 即將出現的 (B) 生活奢靡的 (C) 外向的 (D) 教養　　A

13. The government is going to raise tax in order to cut the _____ deficit.

(A) stock (B) budget (C) money (D) proposal

14. The police _____ an investigation into the car accident.

(A) fixed (B) invited (C) launched (D) testified

15. He is _____ ! He tried to set up his own company many times but has never succeeded.

(A) apathetic (B) empathetic (C) pathetic (D) sympathetic

16. The company's _____ is to provide the highest level of quality and service for every customer.

(A) announcement (B) commitment (C) temptation
(D) consumption

17. Every year we have _____ days to raise money for people in poverty.

(A) giving (B) generous (C) goodwill (D) charity

18. For decades, Bill has been a strong _____ of peaceful resolution. He will never resort to force.

(A) advocate (B) beneficiary (C) opponent (D) prosecutor

19. An astounding finding by some therapists was that extra-marital love affairs may cultivate, instead of _____ , intimacy in a marriage.

(A) enhancing (B) mystifying (C) provoking (D) strangling

20. When designing the building, the architect was concerned more about the _____ than the decorative features. The result is that every space has its practical and unique function.

(A) gregarious (B) horrendous (C) miraculous (D) utilitarian

13. 政府爲了削減預算赤字打算提高稅金。
    (A) 股票 (B) 預算 (C) 金錢 (D) 提案　　　　　　　　**B**

14. 警方著手調查那起車禍。
    (A) 修理 (B) 邀請 (C) 著手 (D) 證明　　　　　　　　**C**

15. 他眞可憐！他好幾次試著建立自己的公司，但從來沒有成
    功。
    (A) 冷漠的 (B) 移情作用的 (C) 可憐的 (D) 同情的　　**C**

16. 公司承諾提供每一位顧客最高水準的品質和服務。
    (A) 宣布 (B) 承諾 (C) 誘惑 (D) 消費　　　　　　　　**B**

17. 我們每年都有慈善日，爲貧困的人籌募金錢。
    (A) 禮物 (B) 慷慨的 (C) 善意 (D) 慈善　　　　　　　**D**

18. 數十年來，比爾一直是和平解決的強力擁護者，他從不訴諸
    武力。
    (A) 提倡者 (B) 受益人 (C) 反對者 (D) 檢舉人　　　　**A**

19. 有些治療師有一項驚人發現：婚外情可以培養婚姻的親密關
    係，而不是壓抑。
    (A) 增強 (B) 迷惑 (C) 激怒 (D) 壓制　　　　　　　　**D**

20. 比起特色裝飾，建築師在設計這座建築物時更重視實用性。
    成果就是每一空間都有實用且獨特的功能。
    (A) 群居的 (B) 可怕的 (C) 不可思議的 (D) 實用性　　**D**

字彙題
22

1. The criminal burned the neighbor's house out of a _____ action, because he lost his own house two years ago in a fire.
   (A) compassionate (B) flamboyant (C) gibberish (D) vindictive

2. After workers had demonstrated in protest at the pension reform, many of them appeared to have _____ accepted that the forthcoming policy was inevitable.
   (A) grudgingly (B) dauntingly (C) passionately (D) substantially

3. Jennifer is considered an _____ leader because she never seeks the opinions of her colleagues.
   (A) inactive (B) autocratic (C) affable (D) ambiguous

4. My friends were supposed to fly home to Taipei last night after spending the weekend with us, but they were _____ because of bad weather.
   (A) stretched (B) strengthened (C) strangled (D) stranded

5. _____ margins have been slashed to the bone in an attempt to keep turnover moving.
   (A) Bonus (B) Income (C) Profit (D) Account

6. In any field of science, small samples lead to _____ results. To find reliable answers, researchers need a lot of data.
   (A) obscene (B) obsolete (C) scarce (D) spurious

7. Meteorites fascinate scientists because they are the smashed-up _____ of asteroids—the tiny planets that orbit between Mars and Jupiter.
   (A) corpses (B) genetics (C) remnants (D) traumas

8. When the leadership starts talking about harmony, it's a pretty good _____ that things are not harmonious at all.
   (A) turmoil (B) upstart (C) indication (D) gossip

解答 22

答案

1. 罪犯出於報復而放火燒鄰居的房子，因為兩年前的大火使他失去自己的房子。
   (A) 富於同情心的 (B) 浮華的 (C) 無意義的聲音 (D) 復仇的 **D**

2. 在示威抗議退休金改革案之後，其中有許多工人似乎是勉強接受這即將上路的政策。
   (A) 勉強地 (B) 嚇人地 (C) 熱烈地 (D) 實質上 **A**

3. 珍妮佛被認為是一位獨裁領導者，她從不徵求同事的意見。
   (A) 不活躍的 (B) 獨裁的 (C) 和藹的 (D) 模擬兩可的 **B**

4. 我朋友和我們共渡周末後，本應在昨夜搭機回台，卻因為惡劣天氣受困。
   (A) 伸展 (B) 加強 (C) 壓制 (D) 陷住 **D**

5. 為了使營業額維持運作，利潤餘額已經砍到見骨了。
   (A) 紅利 (B) 收入 (C) 利潤 (D) 帳目 **C**

6. 在任何科學領域中，樣本不足會導致錯誤的結論。為了得到可靠的答案，研究人員需要很多資料。
   (A) 淫蕩的 (B) 陳舊的 (C) 稀有的 (D) 誤謬的 **D**

7. 隕石令科學家著迷，因為它們是沿著火星和木星之間軌道繞行的微小行星，相互撞擊後的殘屑。
   (A) 屍體 (B) 遺傳學 (C) 殘屑 (D) 創傷 **C**

8. 當領導人員開始談論和諧時，明顯地表示事情一點也不和諧。
   (A) 騷動 (B) 暴發戶 (C) 表示 (D) 閒話 **C**

9. A huge crowd of fans have been waiting in line for hours to get their much loved singer's _____.
   (A) autograph (B) biography (C) phonograph (D) epigraph

10. Sometimes adults have more _____ notions than kids do, so it is more difficult for adults to accept new conditions.
    (A) prepared (B) previewed (C) precedented (D) preconceived

11. Research suggests that there are warning signs that can prevent a future stroke. _____, many people ignore the symptoms.
    (A) Enthusiastically (B) Optimistically (C) Abundantly
    (D) Unfortunately

12. Psychologists have always stressed that learning is best _____ by capturing the learner's interest in the subject matter.
    (A) fostered (B) frustrated (C) distracted (D) annexed

13. When the eyes act in concert with other parts of the face, communication becomes increasingly _____. That's why the eye movement is an essential part of communication.
    (A) implicit (B) intrinsic (C) external (D) explicit

14. One of the great non-monetary benefits of a full-time job is the _____ of friendships you develop. It is a benefit that most of us take for granted.
    (A) accessory (B) controversy (C) momentum (D) wellspring

15. The new secretary would do anything to please her boss. It was not difficult for her co-workers to see that from her _____ manners.
    (A) appalling (B) beckoning (C) gratifying (D) ingratiating

答案

9. 一大群粉絲排隊等了好幾個小時，就是爲了得到鍾愛歌手的親筆簽名。
   (A) 親筆簽名 (B) 傳記 (C) 留聲機 (D) 碑文　　　　V

10. 有時候成人比孩子有更多先入爲主的看法，因此較難接受新環境。
   (A) 預備的 (B) 預習的 (C) 有先例的 (D) 預見的　　　D

11. 研究顯示有許多能夠預防日後中風的警告信號。不幸的是，許多人都忽略了這些徵兆。
   (A) 熱情地 (B) 樂觀地 (C) 大量地 (D) 不幸地　　　D

12. 心理學家一直強調抓住學習者對學科的興趣，學習就會達到最佳進展。
   (A) 促進 (B) 挫折 (C) 分散 (D) 獲得　　　　　　V

13. 當眼睛和臉部其他部位協調動作時，溝通變得更加明確，那就是爲什麼眼部活動是溝通的重要一環。
   (A) 含蓄的 (B) 內在的 (C) 外部的 (D) 明確的　　　D

金榜解析 in concert with 與…協調

14. 全職工作中一項很棒的非金錢利益是你所發展出來的友誼泉源，這是我們多數人都視爲理所當然的。
   (A) 附件 (B) 爭論 (C) 總量 (D) 泉源　　　　　　D

15. 新任秘書會做任何事來討老闆歡心，她同事不難從她討好的行徑中看出端倪。
   (A) 驚嚇的 (B) 引誘的 (C) 使喜悅的 (D) 討好的　　　D

16. _____ in Taipei is becoming much more convenient with the newly built Mass Rapid Transit.
(A) Passenger (B) Traffic (C) Transportation (D) Vehicle

17. Native Americans have a cultural _____ that extends back over 1000 years.
(A) average (B) heritage (C) exchange (D) visage

18. If a professor uses others' essays without documentation, he will be accused of _____ and expelled out of the academic community.
(A) burglary (B) counterfeit (C) ghostwriting (D) plagiarism

19. In his childhood, his family lived in an inner city where parents were _____ by bad housing and shortage of money.
(A) anticipated (B) backfired (C) committed (D) depressed

20. By learning to express _____, to show thankfulness to people, people can become more satisfied with their daily lives.
(A) hostility (B) gratitude (C) intimacy (D) fantasy

考前衝刺★★★★★

1. Mr. Johnson threatened to _____ the magazine for libel.
(A) arrest (B) sell (C) sue (D) allow

2. He got a speeding _____ from the police yesterday, as he was driving at 80 miles an hour while the limit was 65.
(A) bumper (B) flier (C) pamphlet (D) ticket

公職精選歷屆
必考字彙題

答案

16. 台北的交通因新建的捷運變得更為方便。
    (A) 乘客 (B) 交通 (C) 運輸 (D) 交通工具   **B**

17. 美國原住民有豐富的文化遺產,可以往前追溯至一千多年前。
    (A) 平均 (B) 遺產 (C) 交換 (D) 面貌   **B**

18. 如果教授無正式授權就使用別人的文章,他會被指控抄襲並被逐出學術界。
    (A) 竊盜 (B) 贗品 (C) 代寫 (D) 抄襲   **D**

金榜解析 be accused of 遭指控

19. 他小時候家住內城區,因那裏屋況糟糕本身又沒錢使他父母意志消沉。
    (A) 期待 (B) 回火 (C) 委任 (D) 沮喪   **D**

金榜解析 an inner city是指大城市中破敗的貧民區

20. 學習表達感謝以及對人表示感激,人們可以對他們的日常生活更加知足。
    (A) 敵意 (B) 感謝 (C) 親密 (D) 幻想   **B**

考前衝刺★★★★★

答案

1. 強生先生威脅要控告那家雜誌社誹謗。
   (A) 逮捕 (B) 販賣 (C) 控告 (D) 允許   **C**

2. 他昨天收到一張來自警方的超速罰單,因為他開車時速八十英哩,而速限是六十五。
   (A) 保險桿 (B) 傳單 (C) 小冊子 (D) 罰單   **D**

公職精選歷屆 **必考**字彙題

117

3. This particular series of exhibits in London _____ the historical ties between England and America, for better and for worse.
(A) deplores (B) explores (C) averages (D) supplicates

4. The doctor was pleased to tell the mother that her daughter's arm was not broken. He said it was only a bone _____.
(A) frustration (B) friction (C) fracture (D) fringe

5. The introduction of the paper is _____. Important details and evidence are not provided.
(A) thrifty (B) sketchy (C) resistant (D) inconsistent

6. Jenny is very kind to her next-door neighbor, _____ her neighbor is not easy to get along with.
(A) besides (B) except (C) even (D) even though

7. Fat people must be careful because obesity is on its way to _____ smoking as the number one killer in many countries.
(A) progressing (B) regressing (C) transacting (D) surpassing

8. _____ its cost, the office ladies still dream of owning a designer bag.
(A) Except (B) Despite (C) Even if (D) Owing to

9. Calm down! You can't think rationally when you are so _____.
(A) emotional (B) pleasant (C) respectful (D) speechless

10. I can't see any differences between a real diamond and an artificial one. They look _____ to me.
(A) moderate (B) identical (C) hazardous (D) primitive

11. The old man tells his young grandson that life is tougher than he _____.
(A) breeds (B) conveys (C) disputes (D) assumes

3. 倫敦的這一系列特展探索英美之間的歷史關係，有好也有壞。

   (A) 悲悼 (B) 探索 (C) 均分 (D) 懇求　　　　　　　　　B

4. 醫生高興地告訴母親說她女兒的手臂沒有斷，只是骨折。

   (A) 挫折 (B) 摩擦 (C) 骨折 (D) 邊緣　　　　　　　　　C

   金榜解析 be pleased to 樂於…
   　　　　　be pleased with 對…中意

5. 這篇論文的引言粗略，重要細節和證據都沒有提供。

   (A) 節約的 (B) 粗略的 (C) 抵抗的 (D) 不一致的　　　　B

6. 雖然珍妮的鄰居不容易相處，但她對隔壁鄰居仍是很親切。

   (A) 此外 (B) 除外 (C) 甚至 (D) 儘管　　　　　　　　　D

7. 肥胖的人必須小心，因為在許多國家，肥胖正逐漸超越吸煙
   成為頭號殺手。

   (A) 進步 (B) 退回 (C) 處理 (D) 超過　　　　　　　　　D

8. 儘管價格昂貴，上班女郎們仍然夢想擁有一個名牌包。

   (A) 除外 (B) 儘管 (C) 即使 (D) 因為　　　　　　　　　B

   金榜解析 despite=in spite of 儘管

9. 冷靜！你情緒這麼激動是不可能理性思考的。

   (A) 情緒的 (B) 愉快的 (C) 可尊敬的 (D) 寡言的　　　　A

10. 我分辨不出真正鑽石和人工鑽石之間的差異，它們對我來說
    是一樣的。

    (A) 適中的 (B) 一致的 (C) 危險的 (D) 原始的　　　　　B

11. 老人告訴他的小孫子，人生比他所想的更艱辛。

    (A) 養育 (B) 運輸 (C) 爭論 (D) 臆測　　　　　　　　　D

12. A cow _____ in a green meadow often represents the peace of a pastoral life.
(A) greeting (B) glancing (C) grazing (D) gazing

13. The island is hot and _____ in the summer. We feel uncomfortable because the air is wet.
(A) spicy (B) salty (C) humble (D) humid

14. The chairperson's speech was full of _____. Many people thought her language was meant to be intentionally vague so as to please everybody.
(A) ambiguities (B) compensations (C) disturbances
(D) harassments

15. He was a _____ player and never gave his opponent even the smallest chance.
(A) merciless (B) virtuous (C) curious (D) generous

16. What impresses me most when I visited Australia last year was the people's awareness of the importance of environmental protection by making the best use of natural _____.
(A) exhausted (B) remains (C) resources (D) scenes

17. As time is running out, _____ action is needed to stop the disaster.
(A) early (B) prepared (C) prompt (D) seamless

18. If you want to _____ money from one account to another, you need to fill out the form.
(A) transfer (B) prefer (C) inscribe (D) describe

19. Sandra doesn't speak Spanish, so you'll have to _____ the speaker's words for her.
(A) penetrate (B) translate (C) indicate (D) elevate

12. 一隻牛在綠油油的草地吃草，象徵著田園生活的平靜。

(A) 迎接 (B) 一瞥 (C) 吃草 (D) 凝視　　　　　　　　C

13. 島上夏季炎熱潮濕，因為空氣潮濕讓我們感到不舒服。

(A) 辣的 (B) 鹹的 (C) 謙虛的 (D) 潮濕的　　　　　　D

14. 主席的演說模稜兩可，許多人認為她的用詞故意含糊不清是

為了取悅每個人。

(A) 歧義 (B) 補償 (C) 打擾 (D) 騷擾　　　　　　　　A

金榜解析 **so as to為了**

15. 他是一個無情的球員，不給他的對手任何機會。

(A) 無情的 (B) 有道德的 (C) 好奇的 (D) 慷慨的　　　A

16. 去年我去澳洲時，最令我印象深刻的是人們相當善用自然資

源，因他們體認環保的重要性。

(A) 精疲力竭的 (B) 殘留物 (C) 資源 (D) 情景　　　　C

17. 快要沒有時間了，必須迅速採取行動來制止這場災難。

(A) 早先的 (B) 有準備的 (C) 迅速的 (D) 無縫的　　　C

18. 如果你要把錢從這個戶頭轉到另一個戶頭，你需要填這個表

格。

(A) 移轉 (B) 較喜歡 (C) 登記 (D) 描述　　　　　　　A

19. 珊卓拉不講西班牙語，所以你必須為她翻譯講師的話。

(A) 滲透 (B) 翻譯 (C) 顯示 (D) 提升　　　　　　　　B

字彙題 23

20. I feel sorry for those film stars. Reporters seem to follow them everywhere so they don't get much _____.
   (A) evaluation (B) momentum (C) flashlight (D) privacy

字彙題 24

考前衝刺★★★★★

1. Diving near Green Island, you sure can see a variety of colorful _____ life hiding in the reefs.
   (A) domestic (B) marine (C) tame (D) wild

2. Since a separate bicycle track offers a slow lane, small children can _____ around freely without watching for faster bike traffic.
   (A) goof (B) dim (C) pedal (D) swing

3. Depressed people are advised not to use alcohol as a _____ for their problems.
   (A) panacea (B) reverie (C) resolution (D) transcript

4. According to organization expert Barbara Hemphill, a person who is not well-organized enough will _____ 20 to 30 percent of his day looking for lost items.
   (A) dedicate (B) stun (C) squander (D) smash

5. George's insatiable hunger for sweets soon made him _____ .
   (A) adherent (B) compatible (C) obese (D) promiscuous

6. The strawberry looks so delicious that I can hardly resist the _____ . The urge to take a bite is so strong.
   (A) temptation (B) appreciation (C) infection (D) hesitation

20. 我為那些電影明星感到難過。記者到處跟著他們，他們幾乎沒有隱私。

(A) 評估 (B) 動能 (C) 手電筒 (D) 隱私   **D**

考前衝刺★★★★★

1. 在綠島附近潛水，你能看到各式各樣躲在暗礁裡鮮豔的海洋生物。

(A) 國內的 (B) 海洋的 (C) 溫馴的 (D) 野生的   **B**

2. 獨立的單車道提供了慢速車道，小孩子可以自在地到處騎單車，不需注意來往較快的單車。

(A) 出錯 (B) 失去光澤 (C) 騎單車 (D) 搖擺   **C**

金榜解析 go cycling =cycling =go bicycle-riding 騎單車

3. 意志消沉的人不應用酒精作為解決問題的萬靈丹。

(A) 萬靈丹 (B) 白日夢 (C) 決議 (D) 副本   **A**

4. 根據管理專家芭芭拉漢非爾所言，一個不夠條理的人會浪費一天中百分之二十到三十的時間尋找弄丟的物品。

(A) 貢獻 (B) 暈眩 (C) 浪費 (D) 擊潰   **C**

金榜解析 spend時間＋動名詞片語，表示花費時間去做某事

5. 喬治對糖果無節制的渴望很快就讓他變胖。

(A) 附著的 (B) 相容的 (C) 肥胖的 (D) 混雜的   **C**

6. 草莓看起來如此可口讓我無法抗拒，想咬一口的慾望實在太強烈了。

(A) 誘惑 (B) 感謝 (C) 感染 (D) 猶豫   **A**

7. It is our dream that one day we can live in _____ , rather than conflicts and violence, with people all over the world.
(A) harmony (B) benefit (C) substance (D) revolution

8. I wish to express my _____ for your kind help.
(A) attitude (B) gratitude (C) altitude (D) latitude

9. When we heard a big thump from upstairs, we were shocked and everyone _____ up at the ceiling in astonishment.
(A) lifted (B) flashed (C) stared (D) perceived

10. It is very common for students to watch TV or play computer games for _____ .
(A) creation (B) monument (C) procedure (D) recreation

11. On New Year's Eve, this pub will _____ its opening hours so that customers can stay as late as midnight to welcome the arrival of the new year.
(A) expand (B) attend (C) extend (D) observe

12. Do you think it is right to _____ on animals for the sake of developing new drugs?
(A) exclude (B) explode (C) experiment (D) excuse

13. I knew Sabrina was upset, but it took me by surprise when she suddenly _____ into tears.
(A) burst (B) fired (C) jumped (D) managed

14. I always take a _____ after a game of basketball. I don't want to smell bad.
(A) picture (B) note (C) shower (D) temperature

7. 我們夢想有一天可以與世界各地的人和睦的生活在一起,不要有衝突與暴力。
   (A) 和諧 (B) 利益 (C) 物質 (D) 革命　　　　　　　A

8. 非常感謝你的親切幫忙。
   (A)態度 (B)感謝 (C)高度 (D)緯度　　　　　　　　B

9. 我們聽到來自樓上的撞擊聲都嚇了一跳,每個人訝異地注視著天花板。
   (A)舉起 (B)閃動 (C)注視 (D)察覺　　　　　　　　C

10. 學生普遍的娛樂不外乎是看電視或玩電腦遊戲。
    (A) 創造 (B) 紀念碑 (C) 程序 (D) 娛樂　　　　　　D

11. 這家酒吧會在除夕夜延長營業時間,讓顧客最晚可以待到午夜迎接新年的到來。
    (A) 擴展 (B) 出席 (C) 延長 (D) 觀察　　　　　　　C

12. 你覺得為了開發新藥物而用動物做實驗是對的嗎?
    (A) 排除 (B) 爆炸 (C) 實驗 (D) 藉口　　　　　　　C

金榜解析 for the sake of 為了…的緣故

13. 我知道莎賓娜心很煩,但她突然大哭還是讓我嚇了一跳。
    (A)突然發生 (B) 點燃 (C) 跳躍 (D) 管理　　　　　A

金榜解析 burst into突然…起來
burst into laughter突然大笑
burst into bloom 開花

14. 打完籃球後我都會洗澡。我不想讓自己聞起來臭臭的。
    (A) 圖片 (B) 筆記 (C) 淋浴 (D) 溫度　　　　　　　C

公職精選歷屆
必考字彙題

15. Many people fled the city after a high _____ disease broke out.
(A) contaminated (B) contagious (C) copulated (D) cretaceous

16. Samuel Beckett is best known for his _____ reprised 1953 play "Waiting for Godot", about two men expecting someone who never arrives.
(A) ceremoniously (B) centennially (C) perennially
(D) prematurely

17. As a man of _____ habits, Brian usually works in the night.
(A) nocturnal (B) nightmare (C) nightingale (D) nominal

18. Credit titles in a motion picture _____ contributions of those who participated in it.
 (A) acknowledge (B) alleviate (C) delegate (D) improvise

19. European governments are starting to recognize that it is no longer _____ to continue providing wholly free higher education and many are considering charging fees.
(A) charitable (B) feasible (C) notorious (D) unanimous

20. My television has nearly 50 _____ . There are many programs I can choose from.
(A) channels (B) departments (C) commercials (D) confessions

15. 許多人在高傳染性疾病爆發後逃離城市。

(A) 玷污 (B) 傳染病的 (C) 交配 (D) 白堊紀的 　　　　B

16. 塞繆爾‧貝克特最爲人所知的是他不斷重寫一九五三年的戲
劇《等待果陀》，內容是關於兩個人一直等待某個永遠不會
到的人。

(A) 拘泥地 (B) 百年一次的 (C) 不斷地 (D) 早熟地 　　C

17. 布萊恩經常在晚上工作，他是個夜貓子。

(A) 夜間活動的 (B) 噩夢 (C) 夜鶯 (D) 名義上的 　　　A

18. 電影片尾的演職員名單是用來感謝參與該片人員的貢獻。

(A) 感謝 (B) 減緩痛苦 (C) 委派 (D) 即席寫作 　　　　A

19. 歐洲政府承認提供全額免費的高等教育不再可行，有許多國
家正考慮要收費。

(A) 慷慨的 (B) 可實行的 (C) 惡名昭彰的 (D) 一致同意的 　B

20. 我的電視有將近五十個頻道，有很多可供選擇的節目。

(A) 頻道 (B) 部門 (C) 商業 (D) 承認 　　　　　　　　A

字彙題 **25**

1. Many adolescents use the Internet to get information about issues they are _____ to discuss with their parents or teachers.
   (A) innocent (B) respective (C) reluctant (D) emotional

2. In the Cold War, the United States , Japan and other non-Communist countries in East Asia sought to _____ China and to stop the spread of communism through a web of defense alliances.
   (A) contain (B) convert (C) divert (D) dilute

3. Not only does corporate Europe have more fat to strip, European _____ has also opened up the possibility for major cross-border mergers and takeovers.
   (A) consumption (B) integration (C) plantation (D) redemption

4. Polls constantly show that corruption is the top complaint of ordinary Chinese. From time to time, the Chinese government executes particularly _____ offenders, to no apparent avail.
   (A) conscientious (B) egregious (C) ingenious (D) presumptuous

5. While most people prefer quietness, some enjoy hanging around noisy places with a lot of _____ going on.
   (A) activities (B) instructions (C) communities (D) reservations

6. Corruption offers yet another confirmation of the _____ attributed to Thomas Jefferson that "the government is best which governs least".
   (A) argot (B) dictum (C) hearsay (D) mantra

7. I don't think educational reform will work. I am so _____ about it.
   (A) rebellious (B) pessimistic (C) competent (D) complacent

解答
25

答案

1. 許多青少年利用網際網路獲得他們不願與父母或師長討論的
   議題。
   (A)無辜的 (B) 各自的 (C) 不情願的 (D) 情緒的　　　　Ｃ

2. 冷戰時期，美國、日本和東亞其它非共產主義國家利用聯合
   防禦網設法封鎖中國，並阻止共產主義的散播。
   (A)封鎖 (B) 改變　(C) 轉向　(D) 稀釋　　　　　　　Ａ

3. 歐洲聯合公司不僅有更多利潤可賺取，歐洲整合也打開了主
   要的跨國界合併和接管的可能性。
   (A)消費 (B) 融合 (C) 移民 (D) 贖回　　　　　　　Ｂ

4. 民調總顯示貪污為一般中國人的首要民怨。有時候中國政府
   特別對目無法紀的觸犯者處以死刑，但無明顯效益。
   (A)嚴正的 (B) 極壞的 (C) 別出心裁的 (D) 放肆的　　Ｂ

   金榜解析 execute處決

5. 當多數人偏好安靜時，有些人則喜愛流連於有很多活動進行
   的喧鬧場所。
   (A)活動 (B) 教導　(C) 社區 (D) 預訂　　　　　　　Ａ

   金榜解析 hang around 流連

6. 湯瑪斯傑佛森的名言：管理最少的政府，就是最佳的政府，
   提供腐敗另一個佐證。
   (A)行話 (B) 名言　(C) 傳聞　(D) 咒語　　　　　　　Ｂ

7. 我不認為教育改革會有效果，我對此感到悲觀。
   (A)造反的 (B) 悲觀的 (C) 能幹的 (D) 滿足的　　　　Ｂ

8. The weather is too _____ here in the summer. It is very hot and very damp.
   (A) humorous (B) humble (C) human (D) humid

9. The photo of a polar bear with her cub on a melting _____ reminds people of the danger of the climate crisis.
   (A) ice cream (B) chocolate (C) iceberg (D) glass

10. Peter uses "Warrior" as his password when he _____ on to the Internet chat room.
    (A) flies (B) logs (C) tips (D) walks

11. When facing an accusation we should examine our behavior first instead of _____ others.
    (A) blaming (B) resolving (C) counting (D) abridging

12. I do not think that these findings on the brain structure of rats can make any _____ to the study of human brains. Human brains are much more complex, after all.
    (A) appreciation (B) contribution (C) invasion (D) reaction

13. What Mary feared most about becoming a teacher was that she must deal with _____ students and some difficult parents.
    (A) natural (B) pleasant (C) quiet (D) naughty

14. Earthquakes and storms may cause huge _____ to large areas of the Earth.
    (A) increase (B) knowledge (C) damage (D) fun

15. An intimacy with Dr. Johnson, the great literary _____ of the day, was the crowning object of his aspiring and somewhat ludicrous ambition.
    (A) acronym (B) itinerary (C) luminary (D) pseudonym

8. 這裡夏天溼氣太重,真是又熱又溼。
(A) 幽默的 (B) 謙卑的 (C) 人類 (D) 潮溼的 **D**

9. 北極熊與幼熊在溶化的冰山上的相片提醒人們氣候危機的危險。
(A) 冰淇淋 (B) 巧克力 (C) 冰山 (D) 玻璃 **C**

10. 彼得以「戰士」作為他登錄網路聊天室時的密碼。
(A) 蒼蠅 (B) 登錄 (C) 技巧 (D) 步行 **B**

11. 面對指控時,我們應先檢視自己的行為,而不是指責別人。
(A)指責 (B) 解決 (C) 計數 (D) 省略 **A**

12. 我不認為在鼠腦結構的發現對人類大腦的研究會有任何貢獻,畢竟人類大腦可是複雜得多。
(A)感謝 (B) 貢獻 (C) 侵犯 (D) 反應 **B**

金榜解析 **make a contribution to** 貢獻給

13. 當教師讓瑪莉最害怕的是必須應付頑皮的學生和難纏的家長。
(A) 自然的 (B) 愉快的 (C) 安靜的 (D) 頑皮的 **D**

14. 地震和暴風雨可能造成地球大部份地區極大的損害。
(A) 增加 (B) 知識 (C) 損害 (D) 樂趣 **C**

15. 強生博士是當時偉大的文學泰斗,最為人熟知的是那無上的目標—他那雄心壯志和有點可笑的抱負。
(A)頭字詞 (B) 旅行指南 (C) 傑出人物 (D) 假名 **C**

公職精選歷屆
必考字彙題

16. Young people are the future. The gains of our democracy would be _____ if we did not properly educate our children and youth.
(A) embellished (B) nullified (C) rectified (D) furnished

17. Susan won a _____ because of her excellent academic performance. She doesn't have to find a part-time job to pay her way through college.
(A) scholarship (B) trophy (C) uniform (D) proposal

18. We feel great sympathy for the abused child, who has got _____ all over.
(A) affections (B) ornaments (C) bruises (D) ruins

19. Some people believe that it is possible to _____ colds by drinking a lot of orange juice every day.
(A) protect (B) project (C) predict (D) prevent

20. The price of each new product is _____ by its production cost and market value.
(A) reiterated (B) yearned (C) determined (D) inverted

考前衝刺★★★★★

1. We _____ from our parents many of our physical characteristics.
(A) induced (B) imported (C) inherited (D) incapacitated

2. By the inherent rights of a human being, man believes he has the privilege to _____ dominion over the animal world.
(A) contemplate (B) discharge (C) exclude (D) impose

解答 25

16. 年輕人是未來的主人翁。如果沒有適當教育我們的孩子及青年，民主的成果會遭抹煞。
    (A)裝飾 (B) 抹煞 (C) 矯正 (D) 佈置　　**B**

17. 蘇珊靠著優秀的學術表現贏得獎學金，她不需要找一份兼職來支付她的大學學費。
    (A) 獎學金 (B) 獎盃 (C) 制服 (D) 提議　　**A**

18. 我們對這位全身有多處瘀傷的受虐兒感到十分同情。
    (A) 喜愛 (B) 裝飾 (C) 瘀傷 (D) 廢墟　　**C**

    金榜解析 feel sympathy for 對…表示同情

19. 有些人相信每天喝大量的柳橙汁可以預防感冒。
    (A) 保護 (B) 計畫 (C) 預測 (D) 防止　　**D**

20. 每個新產品的價格是由其生產成本和市場價格決定。
    (A) 重覆表示 (B) 渴望 (C) 決定 (D) 反轉　　**C**

    金榜解析 determine=decide to決定

考前衝刺★★★★★

解答 26

答案

1. 我們自父母身上遺傳到許多生理特徵。
   (A) 引導 (B) 進口 (C) 遺傳 (D) 使殘廢　　**C**

2. 由於人類與生俱來的權利，他們相信自己有強行支配動物世界的特權。
   (A)細心觀察 (B) 解除 (C) 排除 (D) 強加給　　**D**

公職精選歷屆
必考字彙題

3. He was obliged to pause and decide whether he would surrender and obey, or whether he would give the refusal that must carry _____ consequences.
   (A) impeccable (B) impecunious (C) ingenious (D) irrevocable

4. The court rejected the _____ of the defendant though his lawyer made a strong argument for him.
   (A) partition (B) participation (C) petition (D) pension

5. Creativity is a much-needed _____ in this old and conservative company.
   (A) asset (B) commission (C) compassion (D) liability

6. What I am going to tell you is _____ . Please keep it a secret and never let it out.
   (A) nutritious (B) confidential (C) sufficient (D) inspiring

7. With a _____ camera, you can get instant results, save the files onto the computer, and e-mail pictures to your friends.
   (A) digital (B) silent (C) crystal (D) patient

8. The money we have saved in this account is to be used for one _____ purpose: the purchase of a new house.
   (A) spiritual (B) sticky (C) specific (D) savage

9. His complaint is just the tip of the _____ . There is a lot more to come.
   (A) iceberg (B) hurricane (C) tornado (D) typhoon

10. Helen's school is near her house. It's just two _____ from her house.
    (A) neighbors (B) insects (C) pages (D) blocks

答案

3. 他被迫暫停然後決定是否要投降順服，或是拒絕但如此一來必定走向不可挽救的結果。
   (A) 無瑕疵的 (B) 貧窮的 (C) 別出心裁的 (D) 不可挽回的　**D**

金榜解析　**be obliged to必須**

4. 雖然被告律師為他作了強烈的辯論，法院還是駁回被告的請願。
   (A) 分開 (B) 參與 (C) 請願 (D) 退休金　**C**

5. 創造力是這家老舊又保守的公司極需的一項資產。
   (A) 資產 (B) 委員會 (C) 同情 (D) 責任　**A**

6. 我要告訴你的事是機密，請保密絕不要洩露出去。
   (A) 有營養成份的 (B) 機密的 (C) 充份的 (D) 啟發　**B**

7. 擁有一台數位相機，你可以立即看到成果，存檔到電腦上，再藉由電子郵件發送照片給你的朋友。
   (A) 數位 (B) 沈默 (C) 水晶 (D) 病人　**A**

8. 我們存在這帳戶裡的錢有一項特定用途：買一棟新房子。
   (A) 精神上的 (B) 黏黏的 (C) 特定的 (D) 野蠻人　**C**

9. 他的抱怨只是冰山一角，後續還有更多。
   (A) 冰山 (B) 颶風 (C) 龍捲風 (D) 颱風　**A**

10. 海倫的學校在她家附近，離她家只有兩個街區。
    (A) 鄰居 (B) 昆蟲 (C) 頁 (D) 街區　**D**

11. My brother is good at sports. He often plays _____ on Sundays.
    (A) toy cars (B) badminton (C) the piano (D) computer games

12. Mary felt stressed out after working hard for two _____ weeks.
    (A) consequent (B) conservative (C) consecutive
    (D) consequential

13. What _____ to me about the movie "King Kong" is the director's
    innovative use of special visual effects.
    (A) appeals (B) delivers (C) detects (D) attracts

14. The team won the game with _____ . The game was finished in 10
    minutes.
    (A) care (B) courage (C) difficulty (D) ease

15. Last Saturday, I went to Yo-Yo Ma's concert. His cello music was
    so beautiful that it left a deep _____ on me.
    (A) impression (B) facility (C) sympathy (D) recreation

16. No one can tolerate his _____ attitude. He always disregards
    others' opinions, considering himself the most intelligent in class.
    (A) hesitant (B) flexible (C) arrogant (D) inspirational

17. This is a great country for tourists because it offers a wide range
    of _____, such as water sports, historic sites, shopping malls, and
    wonderful food.
    (A) attractions (B) interests (C) developments (D) subjects

18. Let's try to discuss this calmly. I don't want to get into an _____
    with you.
    (A) evolution (B) argument (C) encounter (D) improvement

答案

11. 我哥哥擅長運動，他禮拜天常打羽球。
   (A) 玩具車 (B) 羽毛球 (C) 鋼琴 (D) 電腦遊戲　　B

12. 連續辛苦工作兩星期，瑪莉覺得被壓得喘不過氣。
   (A) 做為結果的 (B) 保守的 (C) 連續的 (D) 重要的　　C

13. 「金剛」這部電影吸引我的地方是導演在視覺效果上的創新手法。
   (A)吸引 (B) 遞送 (C) 發現 (D) 吸引　　A

14. 該隊伍輕易獲勝，比賽十分鐘內就結束了。
   (A) 關心 (B) 勇氣 (C)困難 (D) 安逸　　D

金榜解析 with easy=easily輕易地

15. 我上週六去馬友友的音樂會。他的大提琴演奏太美妙了，讓我印象深刻。
   (A) 印象 (B) 設施 (C) 同情 (D) 娛樂　　A

16. 沒人能容忍他傲慢的態度。他總是忽視別人的意見，認為自己是全班最聰明的。
   (A) 猶豫的 (B) 有彈性的 (C) 傲慢的 (D) 鼓舞人心的　　C

17. 對觀光客而言，這是一個很棒的國家，因為該國提供各種令人嚮往的優勢，如水上運動、歷史古蹟、購物商場和美食。
   (A) 吸引 (B) 興趣 (C) 發展 (D) 主題　　A

18. 讓我們冷靜討論這件事！我不想和你爭論。
   (A) 進化 (B) 爭論 (C) 遇到 (D) 改善　　B

公職精選歷屆 **必考**字彙題

19. After a baby is born, its parents will have to apply for a copy of the birth _____ .
   (A) certificate (B) diploma (C) license (D) permit

20. The dead body found in a deserted house has not been _____ yet. The police are searching for clues to find out who the victim is.
   (A) identified (B) motivated (C) predicted (D) retreated

考前衝刺★★★★★

1. Mr. Johnson always puts on a very _____ face whenever his students fail to answer the questions correctly.
   (A) aboriginal (B) barren (C) solemn (D) eloquent

2. It is hard to imagine how people did laundry before _____ was invented.
   (A) lotion (B) detergent (C) conditioner (D) shampoo

3. The new health drink boasts a low fat content, which makes it _____ to girls who want to lose weight.
   (A) attractive (B) energetic (C) optimistic (D) sensitive

4. This accused official awaits decision from the jury on whether he is legally _____ to run for the governor.
   (A) edible (B) eligible (C) pitiful (D) powerful

5. Representatives from the two countries spent two weeks trying to _____ for trade cooperation, but neither side was willing to give the other country more benefits.
   (A) account (B) compensate (C) negotiate (D) compete

19. 嬰兒出生後，父母必須申請一份出生證明的副本。
(A) 證明 (B) 文憑 (C) 執照 (D) 許可證

答案 A

20. 警方尚未辨識出在廢棄屋內發現的屍體，他們正循線查明受害者的身份。
(A) 辨認 (B) 刺激 (C) 預測 (D) 撤退

A

考前衝刺★★★★★

1. 每當學生無法正確回答問題時，強生先生總是擺出一副嚴肅面孔。
(A) 原住民的 (B) 貧瘠的 (C) 嚴肅的 (D) 雄辯的

答案 C

金榜解析 fail to未能

2. 很難想像發明清潔劑之前，人們是如何洗衣服的。
(A)乳液 (B) 清潔劑 (C) 調節者 (D) 洗髮精

B

3. 新的健康飲料自誇含有一種低脂肪物，強烈吸引那些想要減重的女孩。
(A) 吸引人的 (B) 精力充沛的 (C) 樂觀的 (D) 敏感的

A

4. 被告官員等候陪審團判決他是否擁有競選州長的合法資格。
(A)可食用的 (B) 有資格的 (C) 慈悲的 (D) 有力的

B

5. 兩國代表花了二個星期試著洽談貿易合作，但是雙方都不願意給另一個國家更多利益。
(A) 帳戶 (B) 補償 (C) 談判 (D) 競爭

C

公職精選歷屆 **必考**字彙題

6. When Picasso's paintings were _____ in the National Palace Museum, the museum was swarming with people.
(A) exploited (B) exhibited (C) expressed (D) excelled

7. Because garlic extract is now _____ in tablet form, we do not have to eat raw garlic to stay healthy.
(A) available (B) frequent (C) internal (D) technical

8. Not satisfied with the salary, Bill considered either getting a higher-paid job or asking for a _____ .
(A) leave (B) raise (C) favor (D) vision

9. The foundation has _____ a campaign against smoking and appealed to public support.
(A) discouraged (B) prohibited (C) launched (D) mourned

10. When there are so many important things to be done, why does she insist on so many _____ details?
(A) petty (B) vital (C) significant (D) essential

11. Most people enjoy wearing _____ clothes rather than formal outfits when they are on vacation.
(A) average (B) casual (C) mutual (D) slight

12. The government _____ a special force to the jungle to rescue hostages.
(A) dispatched (B) attached (C) scratched (D) dispersed

13. Some people suggest that a bigger portion of the lottery money be used on social _____ to help those in need.
(A) accord (B) earnings (C) reputation (D) welfare

6. 畢卡索畫作在國立故宮博物館展出時人山人海。
   (A) 開發 (B) 展示 (C) 表達 (D) 擅長　　　　　　　B

7. 大蒜精華已能以藥丸形式取得,我們不必吃生蒜來保持健康。
   (A) 可得的 (B) 頻繁的 (C) 內部的 (D) 技術上的　　A

8. 比爾對薪水不滿意,他考慮找份較高薪的工作或是要求加薪。
   (A) 休假 (B) 提高 (C) 厚待 (D) 視野　　　　　　B

金榜解析 consider可接動名詞片語當受詞。

9. 基金會已發起一場反吸煙運動,並呼籲大眾支持。
   (A)鼓勵 (B) 禁止 (C) 發起 (D) 哀悼　　　　　　C

10.有這麼多重要事情要做,她為什麼還堅持這麼多瑣碎的細節?
   (A) 瑣碎的 (B) 重要的 (C) 重大的 (D) 必要的　　A

金榜解析 insist on堅持

11.大多數人渡假時喜歡穿著休閒的衣服,而非正式服裝。
   (A) 平均的 (B) 一般的 (C) 互相的 (D) 些微的　　B

12.政府派遣一支特種部隊到叢林搶救人質。
   (A) 派遣 (B) 附上 (C) 抓傷 (D) 分散　　　　　　A

13.一些人建議樂透獎金大部分應該用在社會福利,以幫助有需要的人。
   (A) 協定 (B) 所得 (C) 名譽 (D) 福利　　　　　　D

14. The audience asked the speaker to ＿＿＿＿ a few terms used in the talk which seemed too abstract for them to follow.
(A) absorb (B) clarify (C) finance (D) imply

15. Danielle behaves herself ＿＿＿＿ .
(A) good (B) kind (C) nice (D) well

16. We just mopped the floor. The floor is still ＿＿＿＿ , so please watch your step as you enter the room.
(A) wet (B) wide (C) wire (D) wild

17. It is a lot easier to use the ＿＿＿＿ if you would like to cross the street.
(A) overhead (B) overcoat (C) overpass (D) overturn

18. If you go to the zoo, do not ＿＿＿＿ the monkeys with bananas or peanuts. Your food might not be good to the monkeys.
(A) allow (B) feed (C) master (D) taste

19. I am not good with number so I found math very ＿＿＿＿ when I was at school.
(A) hard (B) easy (C) useful (D) careful

20. Please ＿＿＿＿ me to buy some stamps when I go to the post office next time.
(A) mind (B) notice (C) remember (D) remind

14. 聽眾要求講者解釋一些演講中的術語，那些術語對他們而言太抽象無法理解。

　　(A) 吸收　(B) 澄清　(C) 財務　(D) 暗示　　　　　　　　　**B**

15. 丹尼爾表現良好。

　　(A) 好的　(B) 善良的　(C) 好的　(D) 很好地　　　　　　　**D**

金榜解析　behave oneself好自為之

16. 我們才剛拖地板，地板還是溼的，所以進房間時請留意你的腳步。

　　(A) 溼的　(B) 寬的　(C) 電線　(D) 野生的　　　　　　　　**A**

17. 如果你想穿越街道，走天橋會比較容易。

　　(A)頭上的　(B) 大衣　(C) 天橋　(D) 翻轉　　　　　　　　**C**

18. 去動物園時，不要用香蕉或花生餵食猴子，你的食物可能對猴子有害。

　　(A) 允許　(B) 餵食　(C) 精通於　(D) 品嚐　　　　　　　**B**

19. 我對數字不是很在行，我在求學時期覺得數學很難。

　　(A)困難的　(B) 容易的　(C) 有用的　(D) 仔細的　　　　　**A**

20. 下次找要去郵局時，請提醒我要買郵票。

　　(A) 介意　(B) 注意　(C) 記得　(D) 提醒　　　　　　　　**D**

字彙題
28

1. To stay healthy, many people are now rushing to ＿＿＿＿ a low calorie diet.
   (A) adopt (B) admire (C) appeal (D) allow

2. Don't put all the blame on me. ＿＿＿＿ I am a troubleshooter, not a troublemaker.
   (A) Hopefully (B) Likely (C) Similarly (D) Actually

3. Dina sips the coffee and ＿＿＿＿ the morning paper.
   (A) spans (B) skins (C) scans (D) scoops

4. Many factors can make one thing transform into another. For instance, pollution can cause harmless plants to ＿＿＿＿into toxic killers.
   (A) deter (B) mutate (C) revive (D) nourish

5. These materials are believed to have a potential danger to people's health and import of these materials is prohibited, though dealers still secretly ＿＿＿＿ them in.
   (A) transfer (B) smuggle (C) reinforce (D) defer

6. The growing popularity of organic vegetables and crops motivated farmers to refrain from using ＿＿＿＿ to kill insects on their farms.
   (A) ceramics (B) particles (C) pesticides (D) solvents

7. The senators reached a ＿＿＿＿ agreement and they will work out a final resolution later.
   (A) contradictory (B) contemporary (C) tempting (D) tentative

8. If a loop of wire is moved between two poles of a magnet, electricity is ＿＿＿＿ in the wire.
   (A) induced (B) inducted (C) conduced (D) deducted

公職精選歷屆
必考字彙題

解答 28

答案

1. 爲了保持健康，現在許多人都搶著採用低卡路里飲食。
   (A) 採取 (B) 讚賞 (C) 呼籲 (D) 允許　　　　　　　**A**

2. 不要只怪我，其實我很善於解決難題，並不是麻煩製造者。
   (A) 希望地 (B) 可能地 (C) 同樣地 (D) 事實上　　　　**D**

   金榜解析 actually=in actuality 事實上

3. 黛娜一邊啜飲咖啡一邊瀏覽早報。
   (A)觀測 (B) 削皮 (C) 瀏覽 (D) 掏空　　　　　　　**C**

4. 許多因素能使一件事轉變爲另一件事。例如，污染可能導致
   無害植物突變成有毒的殺手。
   (A) 阻止 (B) 突變 (C) 甦醒 (D) 滋養　　　　　　　**B**

5. 一般認爲這些材料對人體健康有潛在危險，而且禁止進口這
   些材料，交易商仍然秘密地將它們私運進來。
   (A) 移轉 (B) 私運 (C) 補強 (D) 拖延　　　　　　　**B**

6. 有機蔬菜和有機穀物受歡迎的程度持續攀升，促使農民不在
   農場使用殺蟲劑撲殺昆蟲。
   (A) 窯業 (B) 微粒 (C) 殺蟲劑 (D) 溶劑　　　　　　**C**

7. 參議員達成一份暫時協議，他們隨後會做出最終決議。
   (A) 矛盾的 (B) 同時代的 (C) 吸引人的 (D) 暫時的　　**D**

8. 如果一圈電線在一塊磁鐵的兩極之間移動，電會在電線內產
   生磁性。
   (A) 感應 (B) 有感應 (C) 導致 (D) 扣除　　　　　　**A**

9. I am trying to _____ her not to take the offer but I need to explain to her why she should not.
(A) disagree (B) convince (C) accuse (D) introduce

10. She _____ his ego, at least momentarily, by announcing— to everyone within a ten-mile radius— that he had the intellectual range of a baked potato.
(A) defected (B) deflated (C) inflated (D) infected

11. His tie was pulled _____ and his collar hung open.
(A) loose (B) loosen (C) lose (D) loss

12. James Cameron, director of the movie Titanic, also has a _____ reputation as a deep-ocean explorer.
(A) fundamental (B) formidable (C) formative (D) formulaic

13. Many companies still need to _____ in a recession. If you are capable and aggressive, you can find a good job without question.
(A) convert (B) endorse (C) offset (D) recruit

14. Disasters are becoming more frequent and more costly. But there are steps all of us can take to improve our chances of _____ .
(A) conception (B) deception (C) revival (D) survival

15. Executives love to talk about _____ social responsibility. But on the factory floor, living up to these lofty ideals is painfully difficult.
(A) corporal (B) corporate (C) corpulent (D) culpable

16. In this increasingly digital world, cyber-bullying has emerged as an electronic form of bullying that is difficult to _____ or supervise.
(A) engender (B) intimidate (C) monitor (D) patronize

9. 我一直想說服她不要接受這項提議，但我必須向她解釋為什麼。

(A) 不符合 (B) 說服 (C) 控訴 (D) 介紹　　　　　　　B

10. 她向方圓十英里內的每個人宣稱他的智力只能烤馬鈴薯，至少暫時挫他傲氣。

(A) 逃亡 (B) 降低 (C) 使膨脹 (D) 傳染　　　　　　B

11. 他的領帶鬆了，袖子也拉開了。

(A) 鬆的 (B) 鬆開 (C) 遺失 (D) 損失　　　　　　　A

金榜解析 **loose**鬆的，形容詞；**loosen**鬆開，動詞

12. 詹姆斯柯麥隆是電影「鐵達尼號」導演，同時也有深海探險家的傑出美譽。

(A) 基礎的 (B) 傑出的 (C) 造型的 (D) 公式的　　　B

13. 許多公司在經濟衰退時仍需招募新成員。如果你有能力又有企圖心，無疑地可以找到一份好工作。

(A) 變換 (B) 背書 (C) 抵銷 (D) 徵召　　　　　　　D

14. 天災越頻繁，代價也越高。但大家仍然能夠採取措施，增加生還的機會。

(A) 概念 (B) 欺騙 (C) 復甦 (D) 生還　　　　　　　D

15. 公司的董事在辦公室對團體社會責任高談闊論，但到了工廠真要付諸實行時卻又是另一回事。

(A) 身體的 (B) 團體的 (C) 肥胖的 (D) 該責備的　　B

16. 在這日益擴張的數位世界，網路霸凌已經以一種難以追蹤或監督的電子威嚇形式出現。

(A) 使發生 (B) 恐嚇 (C) 追蹤 (D) 保護　　　　　　C

17. Her _____ opinions and outlandish behavior earned her a reputation as an eccentric.
    (A) auspicious (B) heterodox (C) insidious (D) mundane

18. You can't choose the name you are given at birth, but in many countries you can change it _____ when you reach adulthood.
    (A) annually (B) casually (C) legally (D) ethically

19. TV is probably the most powerful _____ of communication ever invented. It is certainly the most popular and most widespread.
    (A) agenda (B) agreement (C) medium (D) matrix

20. Indians know that the news is bad when the Prime Minister takes to the airwaves to _____ the nation.
    (A) address (B) censure (C) elude (D) rebuke

考前衝刺★★★★★

字彙題
29

1. He is inclined to _____ details. Therefore, his proposals are sometimes not carefully thought-out.
   (A) downscale (B) overlook (C) truncate (D) uphold

2. This _____ device enables people to feed pictures, photos, or documents into a computer system, and shows the cleverness of its inventor.
   (A) biological (B) cohesive (C) explicit (D) ingenious

3. The result of the careless storage and disposal of wastes is the _____ of vectors of disease.
   (A) breeding (B) deleting (C) polluting (D) composing

公職精選歷屆
必考字彙題

解答 28

17.她另類的意見和怪異的行為讓她得到怪人的稱呼。

(A) 吉利的 (B) 異端的 (C) 暗中為善的 (D) 世俗的　　**B**

18.你無法選擇你出生時的名字,然而成年後改名在許多國家是合法的。

(A)每年的 (B) 不在意地 (C) 合法地 (D) 道德地　　**C**

19.電視或許是所有發明中最有力的傳媒,它確實是最受歡迎且最為廣泛的。

(A) 議程 (B) 協議 (C) 媒體 (D) 鑄模　　**C**

20.印度人知道當總理透過電視廣播向全國發表演說時,是不好的消息。

(A) 演說 (B) 批評 (C) 閃避 (D) 譴責　　**A**

金榜解析 take to 開始…

考前衝刺★★★★★

解答 29

1. 他很容易遺漏細節,因此他的提案有時會不夠仔細周延。

(A)縮減 (B) 遺漏 (C) 刪去 (D) 批准　　**B**

金榜解析 overlook表遺漏,可以加接動名詞片語。

2. 這部別出心裁的設備使人們能夠傳送圖片、相片或文件到電腦系統,同時顯示創作者的靈巧。

(A) 生物學的 (B) 有附著力的 (C) 明確的 (D) 別出心裁的　　**D**

3. 粗心存放和處理廢棄物會導致疾病傳媒的滋生。

(A) 滋生 (B) 刪除 (C) 汙染 (D) 組成　　**A**

公職精選歷屆
必考字彙題

4. People gathered in the square to _____ homage to the king when he visited their village.
   (A) pay (B) give (C) make (D) take

5. During the _____ season, the floodwaters covered nearly the whole nation and killed many people.
   (A) cyclone (B) drought (C) monsoon (D) tornado

6. There were indications that their actions were not voluntary, and that certain forms of _____ were involved.
   (A) coercion (B) consumption (C) defamation (D) deposition

7. My watch keeps time _____ . It is now twelve o'clock sharp.
   (A) accurately (B) consciously (C) genuinely (D) considerably

8. With the increasing deterioration of global warming, climate change naturally becomes a key agenda item at the G-8 _____ Japan hosts in July, 2008.
   (A) apex (B) climax (C) summit (D) zenith

9. Conservatives think patriotism is a _____ to the past. Liberals believe it's a key to the future. Both sides should learn from each other.
   (A) conduit (B) legacy (C) patron (D) tribute

10. The Watergate scandal was the ostensible cause of Richard Nixon's decision to _____ the presidency of the United States.
    (A) abandon (B) abdicate (C) abort (D) abridge

11. The leaves of the trees begin to _____ because it hasn't rained for a long time.
    (A) wither (B) bloom (C) sprout (D) grow

4. 國王參訪村莊時，村民全都聚集在廣場向他表示敬意。

(A) 支付 (B) 給予 (C) 製作 (D) 拿取　　　　　　Ａ

金榜解析 **pay homage to** 對⋯表示敬意

5. 雨季期間，洪水幾乎淹沒整個國家，也奪走許多人的生命。

(A) 氣旋 (B) 乾旱 (C) 雨季 (D) 龍捲風　　　　　Ｃ

6. 諸多跡象顯示他們的行動非出於自願，而是有某種形式的脅迫介入。

(A) 脅迫 (B) 消費 (C) 誹謗 (D) 罷免　　　　　　Ａ

7. 我的錶很準，現在十二點整。

(A) 準確地 (B) 有意識地 (C) 真正地 (D) 相當地　　Ａ

8. 隨著全球暖化逐漸加劇，氣候變遷自然成為二千零八年七月日本主辦的**G-8**高峰會的關鍵議程。

(A) 尖端 (B) 高潮 (C) 高峰會 (D) 頂點　　　　　Ｃ

9. 保守派人士認為愛國主義是對過去的明證，而自由主義者相信它是未來的關鍵，雙方都應該要彼此學習。

(A) 溝渠 (B) 遺產 (C) 庇護者 (D) 明證　　　　　Ｄ

10. 水門醜聞是理查尼克森決定放棄美國總統職務的表面原因。

(A) 放棄 (B) 退位 (C) 流產 (D) 剝奪　　　　　　Ｂ

11. 樹上的葉子開始枯萎，因為已經很長一段時間沒有下雨了。

(A) 枯萎 (B) 盛開 (C) 發芽 (D) 生長　　　　　　Ａ

12. Peter tends to be jealous of those people who _____ what he does not have.
    (A) celebrate (B) lounge (C) motivate (D) possess

13. Department stores always draw crowds of shoppers when they are holding annual _____ sales.
    (A) attendance (B) clearance (C) overall (D) terminal

14. The government was bitterly _____ for the new educational reform, and there were heated debates and unsettled disputes among scholars.
    (A) denounced (B) deprived (C) descended (D) detained

15. Two months after Emily resigned, she began to _____ her decision because she could not find another job.
    (A) applaud (B) deter (C) nibble (D) regret

16. Her knees and ankles hurt so much that she had to take the _____ to the second floor. Climbing the stairs was just too hard for her.
    (A) elevator (B) carriage (C) parachute (D) saucer

17. Fanny's skirt is very _____ in design. I haven't seen anyone else wear a similar one.
    (A) ordinary (B) visible (C) ambitious (D) unique

18. Please read the instructions carefully before you _____ the model ship.
    (A) assemble (B) resemble (C) distract (D) extract

19. In winter, women usually rub cream into their skin to _____ it and make it softer.
    (A) mature (B) moisturize (C) multiply (D) motivate

20. ATM is short for automatic _____ machine.
    (A) television (B) telephone (C) telegram (D) teller

答案

12. 彼德容易嫉妒那些擁有他所沒有的人。

(A) 慶祝 (B) 休息室 (C) 激發 (D) 擁有　　　　　**D**

13. 百貨公司舉行年度清倉大拍賣時，總會吸引大批購物人潮。

(A) 出席 (B) 清倉大拍賣 (C) 整體的 (D) 終點　　**B**

14. 政府因新的教育改革受到激烈譴責，學者之間仍有激烈辯論和未定的爭議。

(A) 譴責 (B) 剝奪 (C) 下降 (D) 耽擱　　　　**A**

15. 艾瑪莉辭職兩個月後，她因為找不到另一份工作開始後悔她的決定。

(A) 鼓掌 (B) 阻止 (C) 咬一小口的量 (D) 後悔　**D**

16. 她的膝蓋和腳踝傷得很重，因此她必須搭電梯到二樓，爬樓梯對她來說太困難了。

(A) 電梯 (B) 運輸 (C) 降落傘 (D) 茶碟　　　**A**

17. 芬尼裙子的設計非常獨特，我還沒見過其他人穿著類似的裙子。

(A) 平常的 (B) 看得見的 (C) 野心勃勃的 (D) 獨特的　**D**

18. 在你組裝模型船之前請仔細閱讀說明。

(A) 組合 (B) 相似 (C) 分散 (D) 萃取物　　　**A**

19. 在冬天，女人通常會擦乳液滋潤皮膚並使之更柔軟。

(A)成熟的 (B) 滋潤 (C) 乘 (D) 激勵　　　　**B**

20. ATM是自動存提款機的縮寫。

(A) 電視 (B) 電話 (C) 電報 (D) 出納　　　　**D**

金榜解析 be short for …的縮寫

公職精選歷屆
必考字彙題

1. In a typical school day, when you walk around the campus, all that can be heard are the teachers' voices _____ from the classrooms.
   (A) emanating (B) incubating (C) overhearing (D) tranquilizing

2. I was _____ surprised when hearing about her sudden decision to give up her career.
   (A) someday (B) somewhere (C) sometimes (D) somewhat

3. Looking at my high school year book, I could not help but feel _____ . How I missed those good old days!
   (A) hypocritical (B) nostalgic (C) phlegmatic (D) submissive

4. The Chinese basketball team lost its first game and was _____ from the tournament.
   (A) promoted (B) pronounced (C) stressed (D) eliminated

5. They _____ an old barn into a comfortable little house.
   (A) converted (B) complicated (C) contradicted (D) confused

6. Helen is a tomboy, but the pink fancy dress she wore at the party made her look very _____ .
   (A) shabby (B) masculine (C) feminine (D) fastidious

7. The cause of the car accident was still in dispute. However, some people speculated that the driver's _____ was the cause of the accident since he had driven continuously for more than ten hours.
   (A) exhaust (B) excess (C) fatigue (D) matter

8. In order to buy an apartment, Vivian forces herself to make a _____ of twenty thousand dollars at the bank every month.
   (A) benefit (B) deposit (C) demand (D) routine

解答
30

答案

1. 典型的學校生活中，當你在校園四處走動時，你所聽到的是從教室傳來老師的聲音。
   (A) 起源 (B) 孵化 (C) 偷聽 (D) 變鎖定　　　　　　A

2. 聽到她突然決定放棄工作時，我有些驚訝。
   (A) 某一天 (B) 某處 (C) 有時候 (D) 有點　　　　　D

3. 看著中學畢業紀念冊，我不禁有些懷舊，好想念那些過往美好的日子！
   (A) 偽善的 (B) 懷舊的 (C) 遲鈍的 (D) 服從的　　　B

4. 大陸籃球隊輸掉第一場比賽，並且從錦標賽中淘汰。
   (A) 促進 (B) 明顯的 (C) 注重 (D) 除去　　　　　　D

5. 他們把一間舊穀倉改成舒適的小房子。
   (A) 轉換 (B) 複雜 (C) 反駁 (D) 困惑　　　　　　　A

6. 海倫是一個男人婆，但她在宴會穿的粉紅色洋裝讓她看起來非常女性化。
   (A) 破舊的 (B) 男性 (C) 女性的 (D) 難取悅的　　　C

7. 車禍的起因仍是個爭議，然而有些人推測駕駛員的疲累是意外的原因，因爲他連續開車長達十多個小時。
   (A) 用盡 (B) 超過 (C) 疲勞 (D) 事件　　　　　　　C

8. 爲了買一棟公寓，薇薇安強迫自己每個月在銀行存二萬元。
   (A) 利益 (B) 存款 (C) 需求 (D) 慣例　　　　　　　B

金榜解析 make a deposit of=deposit 存款

公職精選歷屆
必考字彙題

9. The study shows that 36 percent of people are obsessed with famous people and tend to _____ celebrities.
   (A) despise (B) indulge (C) torture (D) worship

10. After several years of training, he has a good _____ of English now.
    (A) demand (B) command (C) diligence (D) confusion

11. It was _____ that he turned in the assignment late. He is always on time.
    (A) natural (B) unusual (C) ordinary (D) honorary

12. Drinking is legal and _____ accepted in every culture. People everywhere drink alcohol on various occasions.
    (A) barely (B) likely (C) rarely (D) widely

13. The best way to protect the leather of your shoes is to _____ them regularly.
    (A) weave (B) dye (C) fold (D) polish

14. She has just been _____ to lead a special committee on fraud investigation. She will call the first meeting next week.
    (A) fabricated (B) designated (C) enhanced (D) suspended

15. She bought her 80-year-old father a _____ health-monitoring device so that he could measure his blood pressure and heartbeats wherever he went.
    (A) considerable (B) capable (C) portable (D) profitable

16. College students are strongly advised to _____ themselves with computer skills while in school. Without these skills, one is unlikely to find a decent job after graduation.
    (A) familiarize (B) identify (C) obtain (D) participate

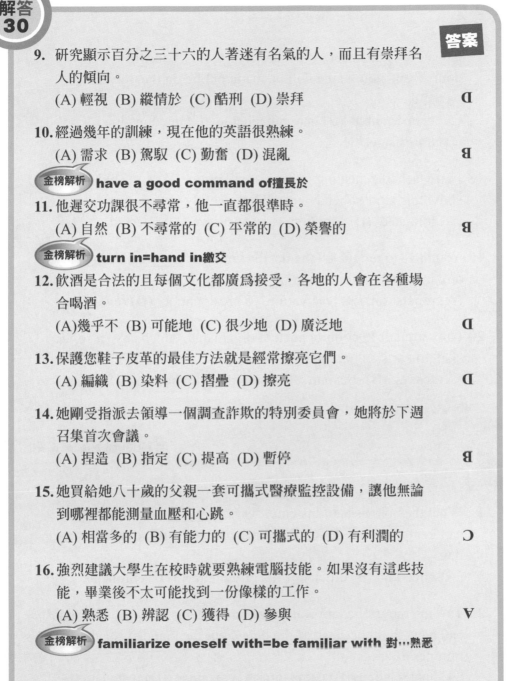

9. 研究顯示百分之三十六的人著迷有名氣的人,而且有崇拜名人的傾向。
   (A) 輕視 (B) 縱情於 (C) 酷刑 (D) 崇拜　　　　　　　**D**

10. 經過幾年的訓練,現在他的英語很熟練。
    (A) 需求 (B) 駕馭 (C) 勤奮 (D) 混亂　　　　　　　**B**

   金榜解析 have a good command of擅長於

11. 他遲交功課很不尋常,他一直都很準時。
    (A) 自然 (B) 不尋常的 (C) 平常的 (D) 榮譽的　　　　**B**

   金榜解析 turn in=hand in繳交

12. 飲酒是合法的且每個文化都廣為接受,各地的人會在各種場合喝酒。
    (A)幾乎不 (B) 可能地 (C) 很少地 (D) 廣泛地　　　　**D**

13. 保護您鞋子皮革的最佳方法就是經常擦亮它們。
    (A) 編織 (B) 染料 (C) 摺疊 (D) 擦亮　　　　　　　**D**

14. 她剛受指派去領導一個調查詐欺的特別委員會,她將於下週召集首次會議。
    (A) 捏造 (B) 指定 (C) 提高 (D) 暫停　　　　　　　**B**

15. 她買給她八十歲的父親一套可攜式醫療監控設備,讓他無論到哪裡都能測量血壓和心跳。
    (A) 相當多的 (B) 有能力的 (C) 可攜式的 (D) 有利潤的　　**C**

16. 強烈建議大學生在校時就要熟練電腦技能。如果沒有這些技能,畢業後不太可能找到一份像樣的工作。
    (A) 熟悉 (B) 辨認 (C) 獲得 (D) 參與　　　　　　　**A**

   金榜解析 familiarize oneself with=be familiar with 對…熟悉

17. Cheating on the exam is absolutely _____ . You will fail this course, and your name will be made public on the university website.
(A) unacceptable (B) unapproachable (C) uncountable
(D) unmanageable

18. In my school, cheating in exams will not be _____ ; students who show this kind of behavior will be severely punished.
(A) tolerated (B) admitted (C) consulted (D) rejected

19. You have to tell me all the details without _____ . Holding back any important information will not do you good.
(A) reputation (B) reservation (C) resignation (D) revolution

20. Only a small fraction of ancient organisms, which have a solid skeleton or shell, are preserved as _____ .
(A) fossils (B) souvenirs (C) storages (D) beverages

考前衝刺★★★★★

1. What the boss asks of his employees is _____ . As long as they can get their work done, they don't have to work long hours every day.
(A) affection (B) efficiency (C) frequency (D) sentiment

2. To Tim, the traffic jam was indeed a blessing in _____ . He didn't catch his flight because of the delay, but the plane crashed 20 minutes after takeoff.
(A) appreciation (B) campaign (C) disguise (D) resignation

17. 考試作弊是絕對不被接受的。你這門課會被當掉，也會把你的名字公布在大學的網站上。

(A) 不能接受的 (B) 不能接近的 (C) 不可數的 (D) 難管理的　　V

18. 我們學校不容許考試作弊，做出這種行為的學生會受到嚴厲處罰。

(A) 容忍 (B) 承認 (C) 諮詢 (D) 拒絕　　V

19. 你要毫無保留地告訴我所有細節，隱瞞任何重要資訊對你沒有好處。

(A) 名譽 (B) 保留 (C) 辭職 (D) 革命　　B

金榜解析　without reservation無所保留

20. 僅僅少部分有堅實骨骼或外殼的遠古生物，能成為化石並受到保存。

(A) 化石 (B) 紀念品 (C) 儲藏 (D) 飲料　　V

金榜解析　a small fraction of 一小部分

考前衝刺★★★★★

1. 老闆要求員工的是效率，只要他們可以完成工作，就不用每天長時間打拚。

(A) 喜愛 (B) 效率 (C) 頻率 (D) 情緒　　B

2. 這次的塞車對提姆而言的確是因禍得福。他因延誤沒趕上班機，然而那架飛機卻在起飛後二十分鐘墜毀。

(A) 欣賞 (B) 競選 (C) 喬裝 (D) 辭職　　C

金榜解析　a blessing in disguise 因禍得福

3. The host didn't even try to hide his _____ ; he asked those uninvited visitors to leave immediately.
(A) hospitality (B) capacity (C) utility (D) hostility

4. In order to cut costs, we must _____ some benefits such as health insurance for employees' spouses.
(A) memorize (B) caution (C) eliminate (D) despise

5. Helen is a _____ . She does not eat meat for health reasons.
(A) vegetarian (B) butcher (C) monk (D) biologist

6. Helen is a rookie in this field, but the personnel manager thinks her intelligence can _____ for her lack of experience. That is why she is employed.
(A) economize (B) extend (C) generate (D) compensate

7. Due to the high-calorie diet and long hours of office work, many people tend to _____ in fitness classes after work.
(A) devote (B) depart (C) discard (D) enroll

8. You have to renew your passport before it _____.
(A) expires (B) aspires (C) inspires (D) conspires

9. Clients pay very high fees to join this luxury trip and they expect complete _____ in return.
(A) impression (B) complication (C) satisfaction (D) occupation

10. The _____ drinking age in the United States is 21.
(A) capable (B) legal (C) favorite (D) popular

11. The search and _____ crew hasn't found any of the tourists who have been buried in the snow.
(A) rescue (B) discovery (C) forecast (D) production

答案

3. 主人甚至沒有想要隱藏他的敵意，他要求那些未受邀的訪客立刻離開。
   (A) 款待　(B) 能力　(C) 實效　(D) 敵意　　**D**

4. 爲了降低成本，我們必須刪減一些福利，像是員工配偶的健康保險。
   (A) 記住　(B) 小心　(C) 消除　(D) 輕視　　**C**

5. 海倫是素食主義者，她爲著健康因素而不吃肉。
   (A) 素食主義者　(B) 屠夫　(C) 僧侶　(D) 生物學家　　**A**

6. 海倫是這領域的新手，但是人事經理認爲她的才智可以彌補經驗的不足，那是她錄取的原因。
   (A) 節約　(B) 延伸　(C) 產生　(D) 補償　　**D**

7. 由於高熱量飲食和長時間的辦公室工作，許多人往往在下班後參加健身課程。
   (A)貢獻　(B) 離開　(C) 放棄　(D) 報名　　**D**

8. 你必須在護照到期之前更換。
   (A) 中止　(B) 渴望　(C) 啓發　(D) 協力促成　　**A**

9. 客戶付高額費用參加這次豪華旅遊團，他們期待得到完全的滿意做爲回報。
   (A) 印象　(B) 糾紛　(C) 滿意　(D) 職業　　**C**

10.在美國，合法的飲酒年齡是二十一歲。
   (A)有能力的　(B) 合法的　(C) 最喜愛的　(D) 受歡迎的　　**B**

11.搜救隊員尚未發現任何埋在雪堆裡的觀光客。
   (A)救援　(B) 發現　(C) 預報　(D) 生產　　**A**

12. This eco-trip is terrific. You'll see a lot of _____ species on the island.
(A) deceased (B) extinct (C) undercover (D) endangered

13. The Taipei City Government has been using Taipei 101 to _____ tourism in Taipei.
(A) broadcast (B) promote (C) convey (D) translate

14. The Statue of Liberty in New York and Eiffel Tower in Paris are both famous _____ worldwide.
(A) logos (B) slogans (C) landmarks (D) targets

15. Let's raise our wine glasses. I'd like to _____ a toast to our sweetest and most helpful tour guide, Linda.
(A) compose (B) propose (C) impose (D) suppose

16. The world seems to be facing dangers greater and more _____ than any known in the past.
(A) threatening (B) broadening (C) sweetening (D) enlivening

17. I couldn't get any of the direct flights, so I had to _____ in Tokyo on my way to San Francisco.
(A) transform (B) translate (C) transmit (D) transfer

18. I like coffee, but I can't drink it because I'm _____ to caffeine.
(A) opposed (B) sensitive (C) allergic (D) immune

19. There's too much crime in that country; tourists may get robbed or even killed in broad _____.
(A) vision (B) view (C) daylight (D) protection

20. When two companies _____ with each other, they become one bigger and richer company.
(A) merge (B) comply (C) haggle (D) clash

12. 這趟生態旅遊很棒，你會看到很多島上瀕臨絕種的生物。

(A) 已故的 (B) 絕種的 (C) 暗中進行的 (D) 將要絕種的　　D

13. 台北市政府一直用台北101推廣台北市的觀光。

(A) 播送 (B) 推動 (C) 運輸 (D) 翻譯　　B

14. 紐約的自由女神像及巴黎的艾菲爾鐵塔都是世界知名的地標。

(A) 標識 (B) 標語 (C) 地標 (D) 目標　　C

15. 讓我們舉起酒杯，我要向我們最甜美、最樂於幫忙的導遊琳達敬酒。

(A) 組成 (B) 舉杯 (C) 強迫 (D) 認為　　B

16. 世界似乎正面臨著任何比以前所知道更大更具威脅的危險。

(A)威脅 (B) 遼闊的 (C) 甜調味料 (D) 生動活潑的　　A

17. 我搭不到任何直航班機，所以我必須在前往舊金山的途中於東京轉機。

(A) 變形 (B) 翻譯 (C) 傳達 (D) 轉機　　D

18. 我喜歡咖啡，但因為我對咖啡因過敏所以不能喝。

(A) 反對的 (B) 敏感的 (C) 過敏的 (D) 免疫　　C

金榜解析 be allergic to 對…過敏

19. 那個國家有太多犯罪事件，觀光客可能會在大白天被搶劫，甚至被殺害。

(A) 目擊 (B) 視野 (C) 白天 (D) 保護　　C

20. 兩家公司合併時，會變成一家更大更富有的公司。

(A) 合併 (B) 應允 (C) 爭辯 (D) 抵觸　　A

字彙題 32

1. If you plan to sue the travel agency, you have to have enough _____ reasons in order to guarantee a successful result.
(A) horrible (B) irritating (C) projective (D) justifiable

2. Whenever my father travels abroad, he always carries with him the doctor's _____ for his heart condition just in case something goes wrong with his heart.
(A) description (B) inscription (C) prescription (D) subscription

3. With the increasing oil price, many frequent flyers feel helpless about leaving themselves _____ to price rises in the airline industry.
(A) vulnerable (B) responsive (C) sensitive (D) irreversible

4. There was a lot of _____ among the executive team members since none of them wanted to be responsible for their failing to get the multi-million-dollar contract.
(A) ice-breaking (B) finger-pointing (C) peace-making
(D) blessings-counting

5. I couldn't find the street I was looking for, so I had to ask somebody for _____.
(A) sections (B) functions (C) conditions (D) directions

6. While English is the _____ language in the US, Spanish is very widely spoken, especially in the south-western states.
(A) official (B) only (C) unusual (D) first

7. Our cell phones use one of the most ___ technologies in the electronic business. No one beats us.
(A) difficult (B) complete (C) advanced (D) progressed

解答 32

1. 如果你計畫控告旅行社，你必須有足夠的正當理由以保證結果會成功。

   (A)可怕的 (B) 惹人生氣的 (C) 保護的 (D) 正當的　　**D**

2. 每當我父親出國旅行時，他總是隨身攜帶醫生開給他的心臟處方以防他的心臟出問題。

   (A) 描述 (B) 碑文 (C) 處方藥 (D) 訂閱　　**C**

   金榜解析 in case=if 如果

3. 油價持續上漲，許多經常搭機的人對航空業漲價難以招架而感到無助。

   (A)脆弱的 (B) 反應迅速的 (C) 敏感的 (D) 不可逆的　　**A**

4. 行政團隊成員之間相互指責，因為沒有一個人要為他們失去的數百萬元合約負責。

   (A)破冰的 (B) 責難 (C) 製造和平 (D) 數算祝福　　**B**

5. 我找不到我一直在找的那條街，因此我必須向人問路。

   (A) 區域 (B) 功能 (C) 狀況 (D) 方向　　**D**

   金榜解析 ask for directions問路

6. 雖然英語是美國的官方語言，西班牙文同時也是非常廣泛使用的語言，尤其在西南部各州。

   (A) 官方的 (B) 唯一的 (C) 不尋常的 (D) 第一的　　**A**

7. 我們的手機是用電子業其中一項最先進的技術製成，沒有人能超越我們。

   (A) 困難的 (B) 完全的 (C) 先進的 (D) 進步的　　**C**

8. The company _____ a 46% rise in earnings per share in the final quarter of 2007.
   (A) reported (B) released (C) reordered (D) relieved

9. The candidates' challenge in the 2008 election was _____: to get supporters out to the meetings and to win over the large numbers of undecided voters.
   (A) two sides (B) twofold (C) both ways (D) duet

10. These paper plates are _____ after use, which can cause serious pollution in our environment.
    (A) disposable (B) disputable (C) disastrous (D) discourteous

11. The loan officer suggested that we get someone to sign for us, since we didn't have any _____.
    (A) collateral (B) collation (C) collapse (D) collision

12. The company leader had not _____ such an attack from the enemy.
    (A) visited (B) violated (C) victimized (D) visualized

13. Food costs more because more people are eating meat and milk products in _____ like China and India.
    (A) economies (B) monuments (C) regulations (D) telescopes

14. When we visit some historic sites, such as the Great Wall in China and the Great Pyramid in Egypt, we can see _____ of ancient cultures.
    (A) traps (B) traces (C) trios (D) trends

答案

8. 那家公司公布在二千零七年最後一季，每股增加百分之四十六的獲利。

(A) 公布 (B) 發行 (C) 重新整頓 (D) 減輕　　　　A

9. 二千零八年選舉中候選人有雙重挑戰：要從會議中獲得支持者，還要贏得中間選民大部份的票數。

(A)兩邊 (B) 雙重的 (C) 兩方面都 (D) 二重唱　　　B

10. 這些紙盤子用完即丟，這樣做會造成我們環境的嚴重汙染。

(A) 可丟棄的 (B) 可爭論的 (C) 悲慘的 (D) 無禮的　　　A

11. 貸款人員建議我們找個人簽名，因爲我們沒有任何旁系親屬。

(A) 旁系親屬 (B) 整理 (C) 暴跌 (D) 衝突　　　A

12. 公司領導人未曾遭受來自敵人這樣的攻擊。

(A) 拜訪 (B) 違反 (C) 使受害 (D) 使可以看見　　　C

13. 像是中國和印度經濟體，因爲吃肉和奶製品的人越來越多，所以食物也越來越貴。

(A) 經濟體 (B) 紀念碑 (C) 規定 (D) 望遠鏡　　　A

14. 當我們走訪一些歷史遺址，例如中國的萬里長城和埃及的金字塔時，我們會看到古文化遺跡。

(A)陷阱 (B) 遺跡 (C) 三重唱 (D) 趨勢　　　B

15. In American culture, it's _____ to ask people personal questions such as how much they weigh or how much money they make.
(A) irreversible (B) illegitimate (C) unconditional
(D) inappropriate

16. Many movie stars have become rich and famous; however, a big price for them to pay is that they lose their _____ at the same time.
(A) privacy (B) intimacy (C) piracy (D) regency

17. After you have visited Hawaii, you'll discover there are great differences between reading about and experiencing Hawaii _____.
(A) firsthand (B) beforehand (C) offhand (D) forehand

18. If you want to explore great ancient _____, you should go to China, Egypt, or Peru.
(A) organizations (B) modernizations (C) nationalizations
(D) civilizations

19. If you try more patiently and nicely to _____ with your travel agent, you may get a good deal on your travel package.
(A) compete (B) integrate (C) negotiate (D) collide

20. If you wish to have a successful business of your own, you often have to make a lot of personal _____ before you can make your wish come true.
(A) complaints (B) perspectives (C) sacrifices (D) accusations

答案

15.在美國文化中，問人家體重多重或賺多少錢等個人問題並不適當。

(A)不能撤回的 (B) 非婚生的 (C) 無條件的 (D) 不適當的　　**D**

16.許多電影明星已經變得有錢又有名，然而他們同時所付出的慘痛代價是喪失他們的隱私。

(A) 隱私 (B) 親密 (C) 著作權侵害 (D) 攝政權　　**A**

17.去過夏威夷之後，會發現你所讀到的和直接經歷的有很大的差別。

(A) 直接地 (B) 預先的 (C) 隨便的 (D) 領先的　　**A**

18.如果你要探索偉大的古文明，你應該去中國、埃及或秘魯。

(A) 組織 (B) 現代化 (C) 國家化 (D) 文明　　**D**

19.如果你試著多點耐心、更謹慎地和你的旅行社協調，或許能拿到物超所值的套裝旅遊。

(A) 競爭 (B) 結合 (C) 協調 (D) 衝突　　**C**

> 金榜解析 **negotiate with** 協調

20.如果你希望擁有自己的成功事業，在願望成真之前，你必須做很多個人犧牲。

(A) 抱怨 (B) 景色 (C) 犧牲 (D) 譴責　　**C**

> 金榜解析 **make a lot of sacrifices** 做很多犧牲

字彙題
33

1. More than one thousand experienced staff members' daily _____ work has kept this six-star hotel in top condition.
   (A) conference (B) maintenance (C) foundation
   (D) investigation

2. On our trip we will only take our tour groups to shop at the most _____ outlets like top department stores to maintain our upscale image.
   (A) generous (B) suspicious (C) conditional (D) exclusive

3. I hate to deal with all the _____ details myself; finding a place to live in a foreign country sometimes can be so much trouble.
   (A) implication (B) accommodation (C) destruction
   (D) reproduction

4. What _____ to see you in here! It's truly a small world.
   (A) a coincidence (B) an incidence (C) a consequence
   (D) an observance

5. Cutting-_____ anti-aging technologies have enabled people to look younger than their real age.
   (A) point (B) edge (C) corner (D) budget

6. Because of the unstable political situation, the stock market _____ to a two-year low yesterday.
   (A) soared (B) bounced (C) collapsed (D) conformed

7. I'd like to _____ you that we take customers very seriously.
   (A) assure (B) accuse (C) assist (D) blame

8. The passengers will have to take legal action against the airlines to _____ losses of their seriously damaged luggage.
   (A) uncover (B) discover (C) undercover (D) recover

解答
33

答案

1. 超過一千名有經驗的員工所做的日常維護使這家六星級飯店一直保持最佳狀況。

   (A) 會議 (B) 維護 (C) 基礎 (D) 調查　　　　B

   金榜解析 keep…in top condition保持最佳狀況

2. 在旅程中,我們只會帶旅行團到如頂級百貨公司這種高級的暢貨中心購物,以維持我們高檔的形象。

   (A) 慷慨的 (B) 可疑的 (C) 有限制的 (D) 高級的　　D

   金榜解析 the most conditional outlets 最有限制的商店

3. 我討厭自己處理所有住宿細節,要在外國找一個住的地方有時會很麻煩。

   (A) 含蓄 (B) 住宿 (C) 破壞 (D) 複製品　　　　B

   金榜解析 deal with=handle處理

4. 在這裡看見你真巧!這真是個小小世界。

   (A) 巧合 (B) 發生率 (C) 後果 (D) 慣例　　　　A

5. 最尖端的的抗老化技術能夠讓人看起來比實際年齡年輕。

   (A)點 (B) 邊緣 (C) 角落 (D) 預算　　　　　　B

6. 因為不穩定的政治情勢,昨天股市暴跌到兩年來的新低點。

   (A) 飛漲 (B) 彈回 (C) 暴跌 (D) 遵守　　　　C

7. 我想要向你保證我們是很認真看待顧客的。

   (A) 保證 (B) 控告 (C) 協助 (D) 責備　　　　A

   金榜解析 assure 人that子句 向…保證

8. 旅客將對航空公司採取法律行動以賠償他們的行李遭嚴重破壞。

   (A)揭露 (B) 發現 (C) 暗中進行的 (D) 取得賠償　　D

   金榜解析 take legal action against 對…採取法律行動

9. The angry employees have decided to take the airline company to court to claim _____ for their physical injuries at work.
   (A) sympathy (B) prosecution (C) compensation
   (D) reinforcement

10. I _____ that our staff members are fully trained to offer their services to the customers.
    (A) oppose (B) ensure (C) convince (D) pretend

11. To apologize for the flight delay, the airline company gave each of the passengers a $400 _____ as a token of its goodwill.
    (A) example (B) sign (C) sample (D) voucher

12. Due to the recession, many companies are willing to provide services at a much lower profit _____ than they used to.
    (A) warning (B) margin (C) visibility (D) penetration

13. The government is trying to make stricter copyright laws to protect an individual's _____ property.
    (A) intelligible (B) inventive (C) ingenious (D) intellectual

14. Jackie may quit her current job because one of his company's competitors has been trying to _____ her with a much higher salary.
    (A) assault (B) intimidate (C) headhunt (D) ridicule

15. Good language skills and personal judgements are important for good _____ when we communicate with others by e-mail.
    (A) technique (B) justification (C) netiquette (D) ambivalence

16. When a company is bankrupt, the company often has to _____ its assets in order to pay back some of its creditors.
    (A) purchase (B) liquidate (C) facilitate (D) upgrade

答案

9. 憤怒的員工已決定控告航空公司，以賠償他們工作時遭受的身體傷害。

(A)憐憫 (B) 起訴 (C) 補償 (D) 增援 　　C

金榜解析 **claim compensation** 請求補償

10. 我保證我們全體職員受完整訓練，為顧客提供服務。

(A) 反抗 (B) 保證 (C) 說服 (D) 假裝 　　B

11. 為了對航班延誤道歉，航空公司發給每位旅客一張四百元憑證作為善意的象徵。

(A)例子 (B) 標記 (C) 樣本 (D) 憑證 　　D

12. 由於經濟衰退，許多公司願意以較過去更低的利潤空間提供服務。

(A) 警告 (B) 餘地 (C) 能見度 (D) 洞察力 　　B

13. 政府想制定更嚴格的版權法令來保護個人的智慧財產。

(A) 明白的 (B) 有發明能力的 (C) 別出心裁的 (D) 智力的 　　D

14. 傑奇可能會辭掉目前的工作，因為他公司的其中一家競爭對手正以更高的薪水向他挖角。

(A) 攻擊 (B) 恐嚇 (C) 挖角 (D) 嘲笑 　　C

15. 當我們與他人用電子郵件溝通時，良好的語言技巧及個人見解對於好的網路禮節是重要的。

(A)技術 (B) 正當理由 (C) 網路禮節 (D) 矛盾心理 　　C

16. 當一家公司破產時，公司常必須清算資產償還給一些債權人。

(A)購買 (B) 清算 (C) 促進 (D) 升級 　　B

17. Whenever something goes wrong, people often try to make someone a _____ so that they can blame that person for what has happened.
(A) guinea pig (B) greenhorn (C) cure-all (D) scapegoat

18. Our advertising campaign for the new Amazon eco-adventure package apparently_____; it scared away many of our target clients.
(A) backfired (B) survived (C) plummeted (D) prevailed

19. People are worried that the Internet is _____ to fraud, especially when their personal details provided online fall into the wrong hands.
(A) susceptible (B) attributed (C) inaccessible (D) resistant

20. Sherry feels it can be quite _____ spending too much time with her boyfriend; she prefers to have some breathing space for each other.
(A) alienating (B) suffocating (C) liberating (D) rejuvenating

考前衝刺★★★★★

1. For more information, please call Paul Stanley at (02) 2422-8769 or _____ http://uoftaichung.edu.tw.
(A) see (B) visit (C) seek (D) look at

2. We ___ you to join us in supporting the Hope Scholarship program.
(A) suggest (B) hope (C) urge (D) warn

答案

17. 每當出差錯時，人們常會企圖讓某人當代罪羔羊，這樣他們就可以針對所發生的事責備那個人。
(A)天竺鼠 (B) 未經世故的人 (C) 萬應良藥 (D) 代罪羔羊　　**D**

18. 我們的新亞馬遜生態探險套裝旅遊的廣告活動顯然適得其反，它嚇跑我們許多目標客戶。
(A) 事與願違 (B) 生還 (C) 驟然跌落 (D) 盛行　　**A**

19. 人們擔心網際網路易受詐騙利用，尤其若他們提供線上的詳細個人資料落入不法人士手中的話。
(A) 易受吸引的 (B) 歸因於 (C) 達不到的 (D) 抵抗的　　**A**

20. 雪莉覺得花太多時間和男朋友在一起會很令人窒息，她寧願給彼此一些喘息的空間。
(A)疏遠的 (B) 令人窒息的 (C) 解放的 (D) 恢復活力　　**B**

考前衝刺 ★ ★ ★ ★ ★

答案

1. 想要更多的資訊，請撥(02) 2422-8769洽保羅‧史坦利，或參訪網站**http://uoftaichung.edu.tw**。
(A) 看見 (B) 造訪 (C) 尋找 (D) 注視　　**B**

2. 我們鼓勵你加入我們對希望獎學金計畫的支持。
(A)建議 (B) 希望 (C) 鼓勵 (D) 警告　　**C**

公職精選歷屆 **必考字彙題**

3. Mayor Ting's plan about the city will have the _____ for the betterment of our life in the near future.
(A) potential (B) power (C) ability (D) vision

4. He is not an _____ person. He simply wants to live a simple life and does not want to compete with others.
(A) obese (B) accustomed (C) itchy (D) ambitious

5. Only when you're well-prepared will you be able to make the best use of every _____ for success when it comes.
(A) result (B) method (C) way (D) opportunity

6. These trainings will _____ you to find a job in one of the banks.
(A) enable (B) cause (C) offer (D) equip

7. Only the members with a gold pass will have full _____ to this club.
(A) chance (B) access (C) strength (D) value

8. The child was in _____ condition with over 85% of her body seriously burnt.
(A) liberal (B) central (C) precise (D) critical

9. The tax cut program will _____ most of the lower income families in the country.
(A) improve (B) promote (C) benefit (D) increase

10. This novel was mainly _____ by a stranger he met on his last trip to London.
(A) inspired (B) impressed (C) input (D) informed

11. Wild Wadi Water Park is an _____ playground for both adults and children in the summer.
(A) idea (B) idle (C) ideal (D) idol

3. 丁市長對於城市的計畫有可能會在不久的將來改善我們生活。

  (A) 潛力 (B) 權力 (C) 能力 (D) 願景　　　　　　　　V

4. 他不是一位有野心的人。他只想要過一個簡單的生活而非與他人競爭。

  (A) 肥胖的 (B) 習慣的 (C) 瘦的 (D) 有野心的　　　　D

5. 只有當你充分準備時，才能夠在機會來臨時善用每一個成功的機會。

  (A) 結果 (B) 方法 (C) 道路 (D) 機會　　　　　　　　D

6. 這些訓練會讓你能夠在其中一家銀行找到工作。

  (A) 使…能夠 (B) 引起 (C) 提供 (D) 配備　　　　　　V

  金榜解析 enable人to 使人能夠去做…

7. 只有帶著金色通行證的成員才能自由進出這家俱樂部。

  (A)機會 (B) 進入 (C) 力量 (D) 價值　　　　　　　　B

  金榜解析 have access to有通路可以進入

8. 這小孩處於危急狀況，全身有百分之八十五嚴重燒傷。

  (A) 自由的 (B) 中央的 (C) 準確的 (D) 危急的　　　　D

9. 這項減稅計畫會對國內大部分收入較低的家庭有利。

  (A) 改善 (B) 促進 (C) 對…有利 (D) 增加　　　　　　C

10.這部小說主要是受他上次到倫敦旅遊時，一位陌生人所給的啓發。

  (A)啓發 (B) 使印象深刻 (C) 輸入 (D) 通知　　　　　V

11. 杜拜仙巴歷險記水上公園是一座可供成人及小孩於夏季遊玩的理想樂園。

  (A)想法 (B) 懶惰的 (C) 理想的 (D) 偶像　　　　　　C

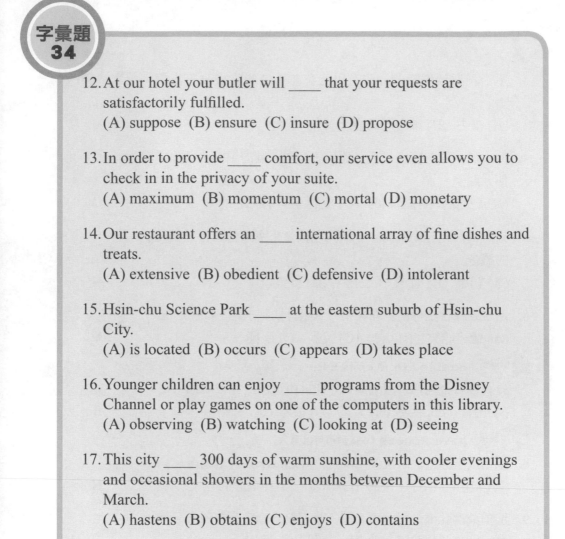

12. At our hotel your butler will _____ that your requests are satisfactorily fulfilled.
    (A) suppose (B) ensure (C) insure (D) propose

13. In order to provide _____ comfort, our service even allows you to check in in the privacy of your suite.
    (A) maximum (B) momentum (C) mortal (D) monetary

14. Our restaurant offers an _____ international array of fine dishes and treats.
    (A) extensive (B) obedient (C) defensive (D) intolerant

15. Hsin-chu Science Park _____ at the eastern suburb of Hsin-chu City.
    (A) is located (B) occurs (C) appears (D) takes place

16. Younger children can enjoy _____ programs from the Disney Channel or play games on one of the computers in this library.
    (A) observing (B) watching (C) looking at (D) seeing

17. This city _____ 300 days of warm sunshine, with cooler evenings and occasional showers in the months between December and March.
    (A) hastens (B) obtains (C) enjoys (D) contains

18. Kaohsiung's temperatures _____ from a low of 14 degrees (Celsius) to a high of 28 degrees in the winter.
    (A) range (B) cross (C) grow (D) separate

19. Taichung City is home to a little more than 700 thousand residents with 64% of the _____ employed.
    (A) consumers (B) business (C) visitors (D) population

20. Taipei offers cheap and efficient public _____ , e.g. its MRT and bus systems.
    (A) traffic (B) transportation (C) vehicles (D) supplies

答案

12. 在我們飯店，你的用膳管家會確保你的要求得到充分滿足。
    (A) 認為 (B) 使確定 (C) 保險 (D) 提議　　　　　　　　B

13. 為了提供最大的舒適，我們的服務甚至能讓你們整組私下報到入房。
    (A) 最大值 (B) 要素 (C) 致命的 (D) 金融的　　　　　　A

14. 我們餐廳提供一系列國際級的精緻菜餚和款待。
    (A) 廣泛的 (B) 順從的 (C) 防禦的 (D) 偏狹的　　　　　A

金榜解析 an array of 一系列的…

15. 新竹科學園區位於新竹市東邊市郊。
    (A) 位於 (B) 發生 (C) 出現 (D) 發生　　　　　　　　　A

金榜解析 be located in / at 位於…

16. 小孩子喜歡看迪士尼頻道的節目或者在圖書館玩電腦遊戲。
    (A) 觀察 (B) 觀看 (C) 注視 (D) 看見　　　　　　　　　B

17. 這座城市有三百天的溫暖陽光，十二月到三月之間每個月晚間較涼，有偶陣雨。
    (A) 趕快 (B) 獲得 (C) 喜愛 (D) 包括　　　　　　　　　B

18. 高雄冬天的溫度是攝氏十四度低溫到二十八度高溫之間。
    (A) 在…範圍變動 (B) 橫越 (C) 變得 (D) 分開　　　　　A

19. 台中市有七十多萬居民，其中百分之六十四是就業人口。
    (A) 消費者 (B) 企業 (C) 訪客 (D) 人口　　　　　　　　D

20. 台北市提供便宜又有效率的大眾交通工具，例如捷運和公車系統。
    (A) 交通 (B) 運輸工具 (C) 交通工具 (D) 供應　　　　　B

字彙題 35

1. Do you know how to _____ between identical twins?
   (A) distinguish (B) extinguish (C) distinct (D) extinct

2. The poison seeping from the factory has _____ the river which is the major source of the city's drinking water.
   (A) contaminated (B) diluted (C) purified (D) swept

3. Water, soil, and the earth's green _____ of plants make up the world that supports the animal life of the earth.
   (A) bristle (B) epistle (C) kettle (D) mantle

4. The film "The Last Emperor" _____ the leading actor international fame.
   (A) earned (B) framed (C) ransacked (D) infested

5. I'm planning to _____ the attic into a bedroom to accommodate more guests.
   (A) convert (B) elaborate (C) justify (D) penetrate

6. When I turned on the heater, hot air _____ throughout the room and I felt warm immediately.
   (A) calculated (B) illuminated (C) circulated (D) illustrated

7. When a complete stranger came over and intended to give me the ticket to the concert, my _____ reaction was to decline the offer because his friendliness seemed weird to me.
   (A) internal (B) immediate (C) triumphant (D) spectacular

8. My brother, Carlson, loves music very much and knows how to play several musical _____, such as the piano, the guitar, the trumpet, and the oboe.
   (A) notes (B) scores (C) instruments (D) compositions

解答
35

1. 你知道如何辨認同卵雙胞胎嗎？
(A) 辨認 (B) 熄滅 (C) 明顯的 (D) 滅絕　　　　　　V

2. 工廠滲出的有毒物質污染了城市主要飲水來源的河流。
(A) 污染 (B) 稀釋 (C) 淨化 (D) 打掃　　　　　　V

3. 水、土壤和覆蓋地球的綠色植物組成維持地球動物生命的世界。
(A)鬃毛 (B) 書信 (C) 水壺 (D) 地幔　　　　　　D

金榜解析 make up 補充
make up for彌補

4. 「末代皇帝」這部影片為男主角博得國際聲譽。
(A) 賺得 (B) 組織 (C) 仔細搜索 (D) 大批出沒　　V

5. 我正計劃將閣樓改成一間臥室提供更多客人住宿。
(A) 改變 (B) 闡述 (C) 證明 (D) 滲入　　　　　　V

金榜解析 convert…into 將…改變為

6. 我打開暖氣機時，熱氣循環整個房間我馬上感到溫暖。
(A) 計算 (B) 照明 (C) 循環 (D) 描述　　　　　　C

7. 當一個完全不認識的人走過來，打算給我演唱會票時，我立刻婉拒這樣的好意，因為他的友善對我來說似乎有些古怪。
(A) 內部的 (B) 立即的 (C) 勝利的 (D) 壯觀的　　B

8. 我的兄弟卡爾森非常喜愛音樂，並且懂得演奏許多種樂器，如鋼琴、吉他、小號和雙簧管。
(A) 筆記 (B) 分數 (C) 樂器 (D) 作文　　　　　　C

公職精選歷屆
必考字彙題

9. In some Asian cultures, people are not supposed to make direct eye contact when talking to their superiors because the behavior is considered bold or _____.
   (A) aggressive (B) appropriate (C) amicable (D) affluent

10. Wearing shorts and sandals to work is considered very _____ in many companies.
    (A) incomplete (B) informative (C) improper (D) impatient

11. The accident was not all your _____. The other driver was responsible for its happening as well.
    (A) concept (B) response (C) blame (D) fault

12. The new engineer seemed to be _____ by the workload in the Research and Division. He stayed for merely a week and quit for health reasons.
    (A) fascinated (B) interfered (C) acculturated (D) overwhelmed

13. If you are so easily discouraged by any _____, how can you ever achieve anything? Hardships are there to make us braver and wiser.
    (A) capacity (B) monument (C) obstacle (D) tolerance

14. If you want to solve the problem now, I suggest you _____ your tone when you talk to those furious investors down the hall.
    (A) tolerate (B) isolate (C) concentrate (D) moderate

15. The library has designated one room for the _____ use of graduate students.
    (A) excruciating (B) explicit (C) excursive (D) exclusive

16. Mr. Smith made such a _____ contribution to the university that they are naming one of the campus buildings after him.
    (A) generous (B) modest (C) minimum (D) realistic

答案

9. 在一些亞洲文化中，和長輩談話時不該直接目視，因爲一般認爲這樣的行爲是冒失或挑釁的。

(A) 挑釁的　(B) 適當的　(C) 親切的　(D) 富足的　　V

金榜解析 be considered=be regarded as=be thought of as 被認為

10. 在許多公司，穿短褲和涼鞋上班是很不合適的。

(A) 不完全的　(B) 有見識的　(C) 不適當的　(D) 沒耐心的　　C

11. 這起意外不全是你的錯，另一個司機也要爲此事故負責。

(A) 概念　(B) 回應　(C) 責備　(D) 錯誤　　D

12. 新來的工程師似乎被研究部門的工作壓垮了，他只待一星期就因健康理由辭職。

(A) 著迷的　(B) 干預　(C) 被同化的　(D) 壓倒的　　D

13. 如果你這麼容易就因任何障礙而氣餒，你要如何完成一件事？艱難就是要讓我們更勇敢、更有智慧。

(A) 容量　(B) 紀念碑　(C) 障礙　(D) 容忍　　C

14. 如果要現在解決問題，我建議你和在大廳那些盛怒的投資者說話時語氣要和緩些。

(A) 容忍　(B) 孤立　(C) 專注　(D) 緩和　　D

15. 圖書館已指定一個房間，專供研究所的學生使用。

(A) 極痛苦的　(B) 明確的　(C) 散漫的　(D) 專門的　　D

16. 史密斯先生對這所大學做出如此慷慨的捐贈，因此他們要將其中一棟校園建築物以他的名字來命名。

(A)慷慨的　(B) 謙遜的　(C) 最小值的　(D) 現實的　　V

17. In Britain, 79 percent of colleges are increasing their marketing and _____ efforts abroad this year. They hope to attract more international students.
   (A) liberation (B) massacre (C) recruitment (D) theatrical

18. Larry King, the host of a popular late night television show, is known for his interview with high _____ guests including politicians, actors, artists and royalties.
   (A) gravity (B) profile (C) solemn (D) tribute

19. He is such a _____ person. He cares nothing but his appearance.
   (A) clumsy (B) damp (C) graceful (D) vain

20. Human behavior is mostly a product of learning, while the behavior of an animal depends mainly on _____.
   (A) instinct (B) response (C) consciousness (D) communication

考前衝刺★★★★★

1. The government may require individuals to limit the carbon dioxide they produce to _____ global warming.
   (A) combat (B) continue (C) decorate (D) inflame

2. If I were you, I would purchase more insurance, just for your own _____.
   (A) production (B) perfection (C) protection (D) procession

3. The controversial singer must _____ 100 hours of community service for altering the age on his ID card.
   (A) fulfill (B) flush (C) instill (D) respond

答案

17. 在英國，百分之七十九的大學今年一直努力增強他們的海外
    行銷與招募。 他們希望吸引更多的國際學生。
    (A) 釋放 (B) 大屠殺 (C) 招募 (D) 戲劇的 　　　　　　C

18. 賴瑞金是很受歡迎的午夜電視節目主持人，以訪問重要來賓
    聞名，包括政治家、演員、藝術家及皇室成員等。
    (A) 重要性 (B) 形象 (C) 莊嚴的 (D) 表示讚美的言行 　　B

19. 他是一個愛慕虛榮的人，他只在意自己的外表。
    (A) 愚笨的 (B) 沮喪的 (C) 雅致的 (D) 虛飾的 　　　　　D

金榜解析 nothing but=only僅僅

20. 人類行為大多數是學習的產物，而動物的行為主要依靠本
    能。
    (A)本能 (B) 回應 (C) 意識 (D) 溝通 　　　　　　　　A

考前衝刺★★★★★

答案

1. 政府要求個人限制自身製造出的二氧化碳以對抗全球暖化。
   (A) 對抗 (B) 繼續 (C) 裝飾 (D) 使燃燒 　　　　　　　A

2. 如果我是你，我會買更多的保險，就當是保護自己。
   (A) 生產 (B) 完美 (C) 保護 (D) 前進 　　　　　　　　C

3. 那位備受爭議的歌手竄改自己身分證上的年齡，必須完成一
   百個小時的社區服務。
   (A)完成 (B) 使臉紅 (C) 慢慢灌輸 (D) 回應 　　　　　A

公職精選歷屆
必考字彙題

4. The new medicine is still in _____ stages and will not hit the market until next year.
   (A) experimental (B) effective (C) exact (D) elusive

5. The _____ earthquake has buried over 18,000 lives in southwestern China's Sichuan province.
   (A) disadvantage (B) interesting (C) devastating (D) discard

6. I'd like to take _____ of this opportunity to thank you all for your co-operation.
   (A) profit (B) benefit (C) occasion (D) advantage

7. It is true that the surroundings will _____ one's work and studies.
   (A) effect (B) affect (C) attend (D) compromise

8. Reading detective stories is one of Steve's favorite _____.
   (A) habits (B) hobbies (C) occupations (D) engagements

9. The _____ from the top of Mt. Kilimanjaro is amazing.
   (A) look (B) view (C) gaze (D) vision

10. Today 42 percent of those under 30 have college degrees—a _____ we expect will rise to half by 2010.
    (A) proportion (B) resistance (C) stationery (D) terminal

11. After 40 years of separation from his identical _____, James Lewis began to search for his long-lost brother.
    (A) loss (B) needle (C) owl (D) twin

12. Fire ants have been a problem ever since they came to the United States from South America. They have _____ across the South and now threaten various parts of the West as well.
    (A) snacked (B) spread (C) squeezed (D) stripped

4. 新藥仍然在實驗階段，要到明年才會上市。

   (A) 實驗的 (B) 有效的 (C) 準確的 (D) 逃避的   **A**

5. 那場毀滅性的地震已經在中國西南方的四川省活埋超過一萬
八千條性命。

   (A) 不利的 (B) 有趣的 (C) 毀滅性的 (D) 拋棄   **C**

6. 我想要利用這次機會感謝你們的合作。

   (A) 利潤 (B) 利益 (C) 場合 (D) 優勢   **D**

金榜解析 take advantage of利用

7. 周遭事物確實會影響一個人的工作與學習。

   (A) 產生 (B) 影響 (C) 出席 (D) 妥協   **B**

金榜解析 affect 影響（動詞）=have an influence on=have an impact on
effect影響；效果（名詞）

8. 閱讀偵探小說是史提芬最喜愛的嗜好之一。

   (A)習慣 (B) 嗜好 (C) 職業 (D) 婚約   **B**

9. 從吉力馬札羅山頂看下去的風景令人驚嘆。

   (A) 面貌 (B) 風景 (C) 凝視 (D) 視力   **B**

10.現今三十歲以下的人有百分之四十二擁有大學學歷，我們期
待這個比率將在二零一零年之前上升一半。

   (A) 比率 (B) 抵抗 (C) 文具 (D) 末端   **A**

11.和他的雙胞胎弟弟分開四十年之後，詹姆斯李維斯開始尋找
他長期走失的弟弟。

   (A)損失 (B) 針 (C) 貓頭鷹 (D) 雙胞胎   **D**

12.紅火蟻從南美洲來到美國之後就一直是個問題。它們遍佈整
個南方，現在又威脅到一些西部地區。

   (A) 吃零食 (B) 散佈 (C) 擠壓 (D) 剝奪   **B**

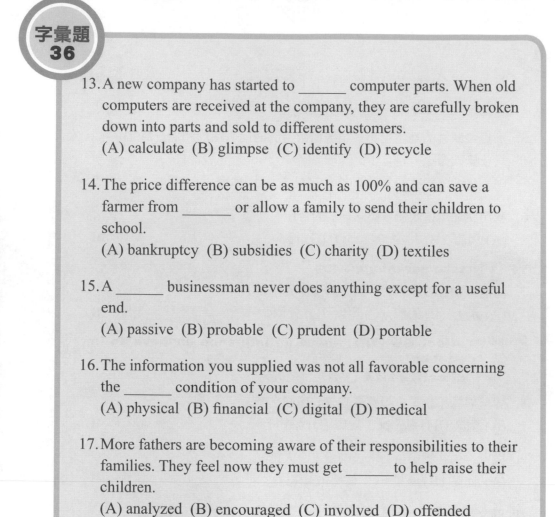

13. A new company has started to _____ computer parts. When old computers are received at the company, they are carefully broken down into parts and sold to different customers.
    (A) calculate (B) glimpse (C) identify (D) recycle

14. The price difference can be as much as 100% and can save a farmer from _____ or allow a family to send their children to school.
    (A) bankruptcy (B) subsidies (C) charity (D) textiles

15. A _____ businessman never does anything except for a useful end.
    (A) passive (B) probable (C) prudent (D) portable

16. The information you supplied was not all favorable concerning the _____ condition of your company.
    (A) physical (B) financial (C) digital (D) medical

17. More fathers are becoming aware of their responsibilities to their families. They feel now they must get _____ to help raise their children.
    (A) analyzed (B) encouraged (C) involved (D) offended

18. Humans are deeply _____ beings. Friendship and marriage make people happier.
    (A) central (B) fearful (C) legal (D) social

19. Successful students _____ their notes after they finish taking them.
    (A) arrest (B) debase (C) hallow (D) review

20. The good weather will _____ all the week.
    (A) insist (B) assist (C) resist (D) persist

答案

13. 一間新公司已開始回收電腦零件,當公司接收舊電腦時,他
    們就開始支解成零組件,然後賣給不同的顧客。
    (A) 計算 (B) 一瞥 (C) 辨認 (D) 回收　　　　　　　　**D**

14. 價差可能多達百分之百,且可以解救一名農夫免於破產,或
    讓一個家庭送他們的孩子去上學。
    (A) 破產 (B) 補助金 (C) 慈善 (D) 紡織品　　　　　　**A**

15. 一名謹慎的商人絕不做無益的事。
    (A) 被動的 (B) 可能的 (C) 慎重的 (D) 可攜帶的　　　　**C**

16. 你提供的資訊對公司財務狀況沒有太大的幫助。
    (A) 生理的 (B) 財務的 (C) 數位的 (D) 醫藥的　　　　　**B**

> **金榜解析** concerning=about=so as to 關於

17. 更多的父親逐漸了解他們對於家庭的責任,他們現在覺得自
    己必須投入協助小孩的教養。
    (A)分析 (B) 鼓勵 (C) 涉及 (D) 冒犯　　　　　　　　**C**

> **金榜解析** get involved to 涉入

18. 人類是強烈的群居生物,友誼和婚姻使人們更快樂。
    (A) 中央的 (B) 害怕的 (C) 合法的 (D) 社交的　　　　　**D**

19. 成功的學生在做完筆記後會複習。
    (A)逮捕 (B) 貶低 (C) 尊敬 (D) 複習　　　　　　　　　**D**

20. 好天氣將持續整個星期。
    (A) 堅持 (B) 協助 (C) 抗拒 (D) 繼續存在　　　　　　　**D**

字彙題 **37**

1. We do ask that you make your reservations right away in order to take _____ of lower rates.
   (A) effect (B) advantage (C) objection (D) influence

2. If this matter cannot be resolved, I will be forced to _____ the contract.
   (A) cancel (B) canoe (C) conclude (D) consult

3. The education of girls is the surest way to reduce _____.
   (A) powder (B) pout (C) pouch (D) poverty

4. We have just introduced our new hair dryer to the _____.
   (A) marker (B) machine (C) market (D) magic

5. Every staff member in the post office must know that a good service _____ toward customers is important.
   (A) altitude (B) substitute (C) attitude (D) institute

6. I will visit you the day after tomorrow, if it is _____ for you.
   (A) convenience (B) convenient (C) convention
   (D) conversation

7. We are genuinely grateful for your long-term _____ in carrying out the building project.
   (A) cooperation (B) corporation (C) operation (D) information

8. The post office announces: sending packages containing _____ items is forbidden.
   (A) habit (B) prohibited (C) prohibit (D) attractive

9. It is _____ to park cars on the sidewalk.
   (A) illiterate (B) illogical (C) illegal (D) ill-tempered

解答 37

答案

1. 我們建議你立即預約，這樣你就能趁勢使用較低的費率。
   (A) 效應 (B) 優勢 (C) 反對 (D) 影響　　　　　　　B

   金榜解析 right away=at once=immediately立刻

2. 如果這事情無法解決，我會被迫取消合約。
   (A) 取消 (B) 獨木舟 (C) 推論 (D) 諮詢　　　　　　A

   金榜解析 cancel=call off 取消

3. 女孩的教育是減少貧困最確實的方法。
   (A) 粉末 (B) 不悅 (C) 小袋子 (D) 貧窮　　　　　　D

4. 我們才剛把我們的新吹風機引進市場。
   (A) 馬克筆 (B) 機器 (C) 市場 (D) 魔術　　　　　　C

5. 每一位郵局員工都必須知道好的服務態度對顧客是重要的。
   (A) 高度 (B) 替代物 (C) 態度 (D) 慣例　　　　　　C

   金榜解析 take a good attitude toward 對…採取好的態度

6. 如果你方便的話，我後天會去拜訪你。
   (A) 便利設備 (B) 方便的 (C) 傳統 (D) 會話　　　　B

7. 我們誠摯感謝您的長期合作以完成這項建築計畫。
   (A) 合作 (B) 團體 (C) 運作 (D) 消息　　　　　　　A

8. 郵局宣布：禁止郵寄內含違禁物品的包裹。
   (A) 習慣 (B) 被禁止 (C) 禁止 (D) 吸引人的　　　　B

9. 把車停在人行道上是違法的。
   (A) 文盲的 (B) 不合理的 (C) 非法的 (D) 脾氣不好的　C

公職精選歷屆 **必考**字彙題

10. Bodyguards were on alert throughout the presidential _____.
(A) audience (B) inauguration (C) configuration (D) meditation

保鑣在總統就職典禮中全程警戒。

(A)觀眾 (B) 就職典禮 (C) 配置 (D) 沉思　　　　　　　　　**B**

金榜解析 **on alert警戒**

11. Japan and France are in _____.
(A) Europe and South America (B) Africa and Europe
(C) Asia and Africa (D) Asia and Europe

日本和法國分別位於亞洲和歐洲。

(A) 歐洲和南美洲 (B) 非洲和歐洲 (C) 亞洲和非洲
(D) 亞洲和歐洲　　　　　　　　　　　　　　　　　　　**D**

12. The _____ weight limit for each small packet is 2 kg. In other words, items over 2 kg are not accepted.
(A) maximum (B) minimum (C) large (D) height

每件小包裹的最重限制是兩公斤。換句話說，超過兩公斤的
物件是不被接受的。

(A) 最大極限的 (B) 最小極限的 (C) 大的 (D) 高度　　**A**

13. The trip to Africa was full of _____ and joys, and we all really enjoyed it.
(A) existence (B) adventures (C) advisors (D) explanations

這趟非洲之旅充滿著冒險和喜樂，我們真的都玩得很高興。

(A)存在 (B) 冒險 (C) 顧問 (D) 解釋　　　　　　　　　**B**